Requiem Blood

C. Swallow

Requiem Blood

PUBLISHED BY
Inkitt

CHAPTER 1: URGENT MEETINGS

MADDIE

I glared at Storm. He grinned down at me from his perch at the head of the table he'd conjured in the alley. His big, gleaming teeth looked nearly as they did in his dragon form.

I can't believe I once thought he was sexy. Not anymore.

In the past twenty minutes of our meeting, he'd shown me his true colors.

Well, since we were in the Shadow Realm, everything was shades of gray. But even in the real Requiem City, Storm's heart was as black as tar.

It turned out Loch's transformation into Lochness had been *all* Storm's fault.

So many innocent people—and some not so innocent—had met their deaths because of Storm's little game.

And it was all to test my skills.

What a cold-blooded prick!

I wanted revenge. But my aching knee reminded me that opposing Storm was futile.

The powerful dragon had sent me flying into the gravel with a simple wave of his hand.

And my knee wasn't the only thing that hurt. Storm's new revelations were giving me a massive headache.

He had told me that I might be the second coming of Freesia, the woman who *killed her baby* to bind dragons within the borders of Requiem City.

And if I didn't live up to her twisted legacy, then I wasn't good for shit.

"In order to know if you're the chosen one...the one to break the curse," Storm said, pinning me with his gaze, "you'll need to learn about those who came before you."

He snapped his long-nailed fingers. A toothpick materialized, and Storm proceeded to pick his teeth.

"Your *ancestry*," he elaborated.

I cleared my throat, glancing down at my hands. We were in the Shadow Realm, but even in color my knuckles would have been white.

"I'm an *orphan*," I hissed.

"Precisely," he went on. "But you are not all alone. I understand that you've met your father, Xander..."

I gritted my teeth. I had no interest in discussing my father with anyone, let alone this manipulative snake.

"My father is dead to me."

Sure, it was harsh.

But Xander was fucking evil. He'd tortured my mates by drugging them and stealing their blood. Now that he'd killed Xythor, just the thought of Xander made me sick.

I wished that I'd never found out that he was my father. I was better off an orphan than the daughter of the devil himself.

"Perhaps to you, little rat," Storm went on. "But Xander is still very much alive, whether we like it or not."

I wasn't the only one who hated my father. He was the mortal enemy of Storm and every other dragon in Requiem City. Xander University was a danger to them all.

"Besides, your task doesn't regard your father so much as...your *mother*."

I narrowed my eyes even further. Anger bloomed inside me.

I didn't know much of anything about my mother, and I wanted to keep it that way. My brother Mason had said she died giving birth to me. That was it.

Growing up at Greensward, I basically raised myself. And I'd turned out just fine, thanks.

I didn't need to learn more about the woman who'd willingly fucked a monster like Xander.

Storm seemed to read my mind even though I still had my mint bracelet on.

"You might be surprised at what you discover about the woman..."

His smile made me nauseous. I hated feeling like he knew everything about my ancestry.

I hated feeling like I was beginning another one of his fucked-up tests.

I stood up from my chair.

"This has been nice and all, but I have better—"

But, true to form, Storm didn't let me get a word in.

"Sit. I'll keep it brief."

At that point, I was too tired to fight. I sank back into my velvet chair.

"Though you have demonstrated some of Freesia's abilities, it's too soon to know if you're her second coming."

"Good!" I shouted. I didn't care if Storm thought I was throwing a tantrum. "I'm not the second coming of *anyone!* I'm *me!*"

He responded with an infuriating smile, clearly amused.

"We shall see," he said mysteriously. "All in good time."

He snapped again, and a piece of cake appeared on a plate before him. There was one in front of me as well, covered in pink frosting.

"In case you're feeling peckish," Storm explained.

I pushed the plate away.

"I don't want your cake," I spat.

He smiled again through a sugary mouthful.

"Okay, if you're just going to eat…" I continued, getting to my feet again. This meeting was over as far as I was concerned.

"Yes, you are dismissed, little rat," Storm said.

His permission only irked me more.

I turned on my heel, ready to leave him in the dust. But then I realized I couldn't leave this place on my own.

Damn dragons!

"Silver will be here in a moment," Storm called. "Just one more thing: I suggest keeping your friend Zayda close. She could be a useful resource in this quest."

My hands were balled into fists. I needed to get out of the Shadow Realm—stat.

First Storm told me that Zayda might also be the one to break Freesia's curse. Now he thought we should *collaborate?*

In a puff of black mist, Silver's dragon appeared. I walked over to her and patted her flank. She pulled me onto her back with her winding tail.

"Until next time, Madeline," Storm shouted.

I didn't look back as Silver soared into the sky and out of their black and white world.

I hoped Storm choked on his fucking cake.

Silver dropped me on top of Req Tower.

She gave me a wink with her big dragon eye and flew away.

Finally, I was alone.

I had the best view of the city from up here, but instead of taking it in, I lay down on my back and looked up at the afternoon sky.

It was gray. Covered with clouds. I could have still been in the Shadow Realm.

I knew I had so much to be happy about. I'd ended Loch's murderous rampage, and now both of my mates were waiting for me in the penthouse downstairs.

Our relationship certainly had its flaws. But it felt like we were all turning over a new leaf.

Still, I felt a deep exhaustion and an unspeakable sadness.

Was *this* why I never spent time thinking about my past? Or my parents? Because it was so painful?

Because the more I knew, the more I saw how fucked-up my history was?

My meeting with Storm had been a disaster.

He wanted so much from me but didn't consider even for a moment how it would affect my life. To him, I was just some pawn waiting to be played.

I knew I was powerful. Hell, I loved the power I had when I sang.

But did that mean I could be the second coming of *Freesia?* Destined to break the curse that trapped my mates and countless other dragons here in Requiem City?

I didn't know if I could handle that responsibility.

Then again, it wasn't worth getting too worked up about.

For all I knew, I wasn't the "chosen one."

It could be Zayda.

I was finding that the uncertainty made it even more maddening. The thought of Zayda liberating the dragons made an ugly feeling rise up in me.

Was it *jealousy?*

I didn't want to listen to any of what Storm had said. I didn't want to think about war coming. Or about my parents. My mom in particular.

But, of course, I couldn't think about anything else.

I sighed and pulled myself to my feet.

I knew two things that could help distract me from all these crazy thoughts...and they were both waiting for me downstairs.

ZAYDA

Finally, I could see!

I gasped, able to breathe freely without that suffocating sack over my head.

As my vision adjusted to the fluorescent lighting, I focused on the man sitting in the chair in front of me.

Xander.

"How *fucking* dare you?" I spat at him. "Kidnapping me? Seriously? How else can you fuck up my life?!"

I tried to spring from my chair, but my wrists were bound to it.

Not only had my *mentor* knocked me unconscious, he had thrown me in the trunk of a car and driven around for *hours* just to deliver me here. To his fucking *office.*

"I apologize for the...unpleasantness," he said, crossing his legs.

"You can say that again, you murdering—"

"Zayda!" Xander shouted. "If you won't cooperate, I'll put the sack back on your head."

I wasn't moved by his threats. I knew he was capable of basically anything, but all I felt was rage.

"I'm not going to be your fucking protégé anymore, if that's why you brought me here."

I glared, wishing I could poison him with my eyes alone.

"The precautions were necessary," he continued, "considering your new-found strength."

He was right. My muscles quaked against the ties binding me to the huge wooden chair. Thanks to Xander's meddling, I still had the dragon strength I'd accidentally absorbed from Xythor.

"I'll be brief. Mainly, I want to explain what you're now capable of...now that you have the powers of a dragon *and* a Blood Raven," Xander said gravely.

I let out a dramatic sigh. Xander loved to tell me how powerful I was. But there was always a catch.

"I believe you are the first of your kind," Xander went on, "so there will be much that you will learn on your own.

"But one thing I can tell you for certain is that the dragons will find out that you absorbed Xythor's power...and they will not be pleased. They will come for you."

"And who's fault is that?" I sneered.

"It matters not how it happened, only that it happened," Xander continued in a calm voice.

He leaned toward me, which only made me want to strike him more.

"Before, your blood magic bound you to Freesia's legend." Xander smiled his sinister smile. "But now that you hold dragon power within you, it is even more likely..."

Xander's eyes misted over, as if he was lost in some dark, twisted fantasy.

"That you are the second coming of Freesia herself."

I scoffed.

Ha!

Everyone at this fucking institution was obsessed with this crazy bitch who killed her own child.

Now they wanted to find her reincarnation? It was more than a bit creepy...but mainly just pathetic.

"You don't believe me," he went on. "But let me assure you, I am not the only one who believes that upon her return, the dragons and mortals of Requiem will clash in a war that could destroy us all. If the dragons get to you first, I hate to think of what they could do to you..."

His last phrase made my stomach flip uncomfortably.

Sure, I had been in love with a dragon.

But that didn't mean I didn't know how dangerous they could be. How much you didn't want a dragon as an enemy.

I'd seen how the Dobrzycka twins treated Maddie. Not to mention the horrifying images of Lochness' victims in the media.

"I have an offer," Xander told me, seemingly concluding his speech. "If you let *me* protect you, I can promise you something that no one could refuse..."

CHAPTER 2: BLOODY AND RARE

ZAYDA

There is *nothing* that would make me agree to work with you again! My words dripped with contempt. Every second that passed in his office made me more claustrophobic, more livid.

Though I couldn't deny that his speech made me nervous.

I had absorbed Xythor's powers. The dragons would find out.

And then they would come for me.

I'd even been so stupid as to tell Maddie what had happened.

I needed a friend so badly that I hadn't even considered the consequences.

No way would she keep my secret from her mates...

If I had to pay for my stupidity, so be it. But I would face it alone. As far as possible from Xander and his fucked-up university.

"Zayda, I know there is *one* thing that will convince you." Xander smiled wickedly. "Just like that panacea was a special project of your own," he began, "I kept something from you too."

I glared.

"Using simple methods, I have discovered an ingenious process... with life-altering results."

I struggled with my bonds, but Xander pretended not to notice.

Instead, he raised his voice.

"I can bring dragons back from the dead."

What?!

My heart skipped a beat, but I didn't let my face betray my surprise.

"As long as I have a sample of blood, I can resurrect them."

"You don't have Xythor's blood—"

"No, I don't, Zayda. But you do."

The awful truth hit me. Since I had absorbed Xythor's power, his blood coursed through my veins alongside mine.

Xander leaned toward me and went in for the kill.

"I can bring back Xythor. But only if you'll agree to help me."

Rage filled me so completely that I felt like my skin was burning.

It was hard for me to see straight as I contemplated this devil's bargain.

I was lost in memories of my lover's fingers tracing down my spine, the way his eyes lit up when I entered a room...

I knew I'd never have love like that again.

Unless it was with Xythor.

How could I say no to having Xythor back? But how could I ever work with Xander again?

Xander rose and approached me, unlocking the chains on my wrists with a small key.

"If you would like, you may leave of your own free will..."

But I was rooted to the chair. Even without the bonds, I was still trapped.

"You have three days to make a decision. But know that I will not make this offer again."

I was overcome by the most powerful desire—the longing for lost love. My time with Xythor had been so short.

And for more time...I would do anything.

I glared at the mad scientist. The man I detested more than

anything, who represented to me evil itself.

But how could I refuse him?

MADDIE

"Hey!" I shrieked.

I felt a sharp sting on my butt. I turned to find Loch with a metal spatula in his hand, his green eyes shining.

Predictable.

I charged as if I would tackle him, but he deflected my advance with a small wave of his hand.

I caught myself with my back against the kitchen island.

"Don't you have something to do other than torment me?" I asked, rolling my eyes.

Loch came so close to me that I could smell his breath. I felt the heat from his perfect chest under his white T-shirt.

"Yes, I'm making dinner," he growled. "New York Strip. Extra rare."

I smiled at him under my long lashes.

"Medium rare for me, please," I requested innocently.

But Loch slammed down his palms on the island, trapping me between his arms.

"Have we taught you nothing, mouse?" he hissed.

I shrieked and wiggled down, trying to escape his hulking form.

I managed to sneak through his legs, but when I stood again, I was facing a nearly identical chiseled chest clad in another white T-shirt.

Hael.

"I hear you're being a bad little rat," he smirked.

"Oh, the *worst,*" I replied, mirroring my mates' sinister tones.

Faster than lightning, Hael reached for my waist and dug into my sides, tickling me.

I shrieked, but I knew there was no escape.

I sank to the kitchen floor, squirming under Hael's relentless touch. And when I looked up, I saw Loch standing beside him.

And he was also reaching down, right for my most sensitive tickle spot...my knees...

"Noooo!" I wailed, before I lost my voice in a fit of laughter.

I writhed around on the ground, kicking wildly, but none deterred my mates.

"How did you—know about—my knees?!" I asked, gasping for breath as I clawed against the floor.

I was still wearing my mint bracelet, after all. My mates couldn't read my mind.

"As if we don't know *everything* about your body, little pet," Hael said seductively.

I tried to be tough, but they soon had me whimpering.

Because slowly their touches were changing from jabbing tickles to sensuous holds.

Loch pressed my shoulders into the ground so that my chest rose into the air with my ragged breath.

Hael separated my legs, turning them outward before pressing them down. Beneath my thin shorts, my sex was open and quivering with anticipation.

Hael leaned down until his nose almost touched me and breathed in.

"Ohhh!" I cried.

"Mmmmmmm," he growled.

I wanted to squirm, but I was pinned to the marble kitchen floor.

Loch's hands moved to my collarbone, massaging the tender muscles beneath before tracing down my sternum, between my breasts.

I was only wearing a flimsy tank, and the brothers watched my nipples immediately harden.

Loch scooped one breast and then the other from my shirt with one hand.

My breath caught at being exposed before my mates—a sensation I might never get used to.

Hael ran a finger over the center of me. I knew I had already soaked through my shorts.

I opened like a flower beneath their touch.

Returning his hands to hold my shoulders, Loch began nibbling and lapping at one of my nipples, making me shudder.

Hael, well aware of my desperation, tore apart my shorts at the seam.

I felt his warm breath on my exposed core as he leaned before me, holding down my legs.

His tongue darted lightly over my clitoris, and I arched my spine. I wanted to grind my body against him, but I was stuck in place.

Loch covered my nipple with his mouth, sucking and nibbling as Hael's soft lips kissed my sex. His tongue ran lap after lap around my clit.

They knew I liked when they were rough.

They knew everything I liked, and they wanted to make sure I knew it too.

Finally, when I couldn't handle the teasing any longer, Hael pressed the tip of his tongue directly to my bud...

The sudden pressure made my orgasm wind up like a spring inside me...

I was about to cum. And both of my mates knew it.

Loch bit my nipple hard as I released. The combined sensations made me scream, bucking into Hael's mouth.

I sighed as the brothers returned to their feet.

Loch headed to the stove as I lay on the floor like a rag doll.

"You guys need to buy me some new clothes," I said. "All of mine get torn apart."

"We'll see about that, street rat. Wouldn't want you getting spoiled," Hael said, looking down at me with his hands on his hips.

"Fuck!" Loch shouted. He was standing at the counter, slicing into a steak on a plate.

"What?!" I asked, hopping to my feet.

"I overcooked the steak," he pouted.

"Uh, that looks rare to me," I said, staring at the red center and the blood leaking out.

It had only taken the brothers mere minutes to make me cum, but apparently even that was too long.

Loch lifted the plate tenderly...and then sent it sailing into the far kitchen wall.

Smash!

"Woah!" I gasped. "What did you do that for?"

"It was inedible, mouse," Loch explained as he looked at my naked body like I was, conversely, very edible.

There was steak juice dripping down the white wall.

"Hmmm," I replied, reaching for another fine china plate. "Well, that's too bad!"

I sent it spinning like a frisbee and crashing after the first.

And I had to admit, it was quite the rush.

I shrieked as Hael grabbed my waist, pulling me toward him.

"Naughty mouse," he growled in my ear. "You think you can do whatever we do?"

"Um, yes," I replied honestly.

Hael sent another plate soaring. I turned and punched him in the chest, and then Loch came at me from behind...

And before I knew it, we were all on the kitchen floor once again.

Hael's head was resting on my stomach when it let out a low rumble.

"You're insatiable, Madeline," Loch said with a smirk. "Okay, let's go out for dinner."

STORM

As I touched down on Req Tower, I grabbed the edge of the tall building in my talons and fanned my wings to stabilize my massive dragon form.

It was true that I hardly ever left the Shadow Realm. I preferred that black and white world to the cold streets of Requiem City.

But after my time with Madeline, I knew I needed to investigate.

I went into our meeting knowing that Madeline was strong-willed. *Spunky,* to say the least.

But she did not take well to my hypothesis.

If she *was* the second coming of Freesia, she would have to accept her fate willingly.

And I was beginning to understand that there were few things that Madeline did willingly...

I huffed smoke from my snout, focusing my hawk-like eyes down into the city in search of the other young woman.

The other potential reincarnation of Freesia.

The one who might be able to save us all.

Zayda.

Though I was uncertain about the prospect.

She was a Blood Raven. Mages and dragons had been mortal foes since the beginning of time. To me, it was rather curious that her dragon lover had met an untimely death...

Just then, I caught sight of her.

It was a rather unlikely location, though I admit it was the first place my powerful intuition pointed me:

Xander University.

The young mage stood with her arms crossed, staring intently at the chapel that I knew held Freesia's Rock...

Could it be that Zayda already knew about her potential connection to the one who had cursed us all?

If she stood on the grounds at all, she was associated with the university. With Xander himself. Therefore, she could not be trusted.

Or could she?

Very curious, indeed.

I would definitely need to keep a closer eye on this one...

CHAPTER 3: PHILANTHROPY IS SEXY

MADDIE

"Wait until you see this, mouse!" Loch called from the end of the long hallway. I chased after him, practically giddy.

I burst into the room to see that the sex dungeon had been transformed into a gym.

Treadmills lined one wall. The center of the room was covered with mats for workout classes. And on the other side, punching bags hung from the wall.

"Sick!" I cried. "But where did the other...equipment go?"

Since Loch stopped being *Lochness,* my mates had spent almost all day, every day, converting their mansion into an orphanage. And the grand opening was *today.*

My heart swelled with pride as I gazed into Loch's green eyes. The red was gone, and so was the monster he had been.

"We moved them to the treasure room in the penthouse," he said with a wink.

"Perfect," I replied.

Upstairs, I found Hael arranging teddy bears on each of the bunk beds in the room for young children.

"Oh my God," I sighed. My heart was literally bursting.

"I didn't know you were so...sweet."

Hael came over and wrapped me in his arms.

"We've always had a soft spot for kids, Maddie. You know that."

He kissed the top of my head, and I practically melted into a puddle.

"Let's show her the best part," Loch called to Hael from the doorway.

I followed my mates as they led me past the rooms filled with bunk beds.

I peeked into each one, my excitement growing with every step I took.

Loch and Hael had created a beautiful space for the orphans of Req City.

Nothing like the dingy shithole where I had grown up.

A nice place would make a *huge* difference. The kids would feel cared for. They would know that they were worthy of nice things.

Of the amazing things they could accomplish, I thought, remembering my own rags to riches story.

At the end of the hall, there was a wall of windows. I stood between my mates and looked down into the enormous backyard.

I gasped.

The garden was still on the left, but on the right was the coolest playground I'd ever seen. The glittering, chrome structure had at least four different levels. Slides went down from every platform, and a ring of monkey bars wrapped around the whole thing.

"Wow," I whispered.

"Cool, right?" Hael asked.

"And we had a mountaineer create hiking trails through the forest, since we own hundreds of acres around here," Loch added.

"Wow!" I gazed up at my mates. In that moment, I couldn't have been more in love with them.

Ever since Hael and I had defeated Lochness, I'd noticed a change in my mates. With the monster gone, it seemed like they were finally embracing their humanity.

They smiled down at me and pulled me into a giant bearhug.

A voice rang out from the top of the stairs.

"The kids are here!" their sister Adara shouted.

I had been more than surprised that Adara was willing to sacrifice her country home for the greater good, but it turned out that even that cold bitch had some warmth in her heart for children. Maybe it was a dragon thing.

Holding one of Loch's and one of Hael's hands in each of mine, we headed to the ribbon cutting.

I bounded over the bottom step of the grand staircase into the marble entrance hall.

"Someone's happy," Adara sneered.

She was right. The orphans of Requiem City finally had a beautiful place to live.

And that made me *very* happy.

I noticed a leather leash in Adara's hand, and I thoughtlessly followed the length over the white marble with my eyes...

"Oh my God!" I shrieked.

At the other end of the leash was none other than *Darren.*

He was on all fours, wearing an outfit made entirely of black latex.

I ran over to him.

"What the *fuck,* Darren?!" I asked. Last time I had seen the guy, he was being torn apart by Lochness. "I thought you were over this shit!"

He just smiled up at me. I noticed he was wearing a thick patent leather collar.

"I don't think I'll ever be over it, Maddie," he replied. Adara's stilettos clicked over the floor, and Darren looked up at her like a drooling puppy.

I rolled my eyes. Adara got down next to him and kissed his cheek with genuine affection.

Huh. Maybe all of the Dobrzycka siblings are changing...

She pulled a ball gag from her purse and fastened it around Darren's head.

Okay. Maybe not.

"We have to get out of here," she ordered. "Go wait for me by the start of the walking trail."

Darren nodded obediently. Adara slapped his ass, letting the leash fall from her hand as he scampered out of the room, still on all fours.

I nearly wretched.

"Maddie!" Loch called through the open front door.

I ran to take my place between my mates. I immediately forgot about whatever twisted game Darren and Adara were playing as I stared out at nearly a hundred smiling faces.

These were the orphans who would be moving into the mansion.

Of course, I wasn't the sentimental type. I was hard as nails. I couldn't remember the last time I had cried.

But looking out at those young people, at the hope in their small faces, my eyes prickled with tears.

As Loch handed me the scissors to cut the huge, red ribbon, I felt my heart bursting with pride and love.

LOCH

I couldn't take my eyes off her.

Maddie looked fucking adorable with those scissors in her hands. Philanthropy was a good look on her.

And I had to admit, even my cold-blooded heart warmed to think that I was part of her happiness.

Of course turning the mansion into an orphanage was a pretty obvious step.

But not exactly for the reasons Maddie might have assumed...

Hael: Brother.

Hael: What about that one over there?

Loch: Spiky hair?

Hael: Yes.

Loch: Very interesting...

I eyed the teenage boy. He towered over the orphans around him. He had a strong, solid build.

Unlike all of the other excited children, his expression was flat.

Maybe he could be our first recruit...

I met my brother's gaze, and he gestured to Maddie. Her eyes shone with emotion as she held the open scissors.

"I was an orphan," she began, "just like you guys!"

What a cute little pet.

"And I just want you to know that you *all* deserve a beautiful place to live! You deserve care! And opportunities!"

The orphans watched her intently. I hadn't anticipated that Maddie would want to connect with them in this way, but it was sweet.

And it was working. They looked up at her like she was a superhero.

"Okay, that's all," she said. "Welcome to your new home!"

And then Maddie cut the ribbon, and the orphans ran into the mansion.

ANEURIN

"Welcome to your new home!" Silver shouted as we entered the clearing.

"Uh..." Dane stammered.

I raised my eyebrows at him. As usual, we were thinking the same thing.

We were in the middle of the woods. Literally the middle of nowhere.

Why had Silver taken it upon herself to find us a new place to live?

And why was it *here?*

"I know what you're thinking," Silver continued, "but you'll find that the great outdoors suits your new lifestyle. Or, your old one..."

"Old one?" I questioned. Silver's only answer was her cryptic smile.

What was she talking about? Dane and I had never lived anywhere like this. Not in this lifetime, at least.

We were in a beautiful meadow with wildflowers that swayed in the breeze. I could hear the babbling stream full of fish swimming in the pristine waters to the right.

Thick-trunked trees surrounded the clearing, giving it near-complete cover.

It sure beat the streets of the Skeleton Quarter.

But still...there was nothing here. No grocery stores. No people. No WiFi.

"I know we were homeless and all," Dane said, "but that doesn't mean we're ready for...this." He gestured to the great outdoors.

"I know, I know," Silver said with a dismissive wave of her hand. "But I set up some hammocks for you guys..." She led us into the trees and pointed up. Two huge hammocks swung between the branches.

"And out here, you have the space and *privacy* to practice shifting. You can strengthen your twin bond! Plus, you'll be away from the temptations of the Quarter..."

She went on. "And if you need anything, you can send a smoke signal, and I'll be able to see it."

I looked at Dane. He shrugged.

The hammocks were pretty fuckin' cool.

And I was already thinking of things we could add to the site.

A rope swing into the stream basin, a fire pit in the clearing to cook our meals...

Dane: A rope swing? Oh, fuck yeah!

Aneurin: Yeah.

Aneurin: Maybe this won't be so bad after all.

Dane: You read my mind, brother.

I turned back to Silver.

"You know," I said, "I'm warming up to the idea."

"I wouldn't mind getting out of the Quarter," Dane added.

She beamed at us.

"Good! There's a lot of talk in the Shadow Realm about changes coming to Requiem...and when they do, all of us dragons need to be ready."

My brow furrowed.

What did that mean? What changes? And how many of us were there?

There was so much I needed to learn.

Silver seemed like she was ready to leave. "You really do have everything you need," she assured us.

I considered this. My brother and I both loved to fish. With the stream, we could be totally self-sustainable.

I flung my pack onto the ground. It had all my meager earthly possessions inside.

A few pairs of clothes, a few crumpled bills.

Enough to start over.

"Thanks, Silver," I said, meaning it.

She nodded once before mist appeared at her feet and she instantly shifted into her dragon.

She makes it look so easy.

I followed her until she was just a speck in the sky.

I knew she had done us a favor, but I also knew it wasn't totally selfless.

What did that dragon have up her sleeve?

CHAPTER 4: CHARITY AND REVENGE

MADDIE

The next day, I skipped up the steps of the new Requiem City Orphanage. AKA the insanely gorgeous Dobrzycka mansion. The new residents had had time to settle in, but I was here to make some big changes.

Ah, revenge.

Nothing could ever be so sweet.

I prowled through the marble hall, which resounded with the joyful sounds of children playing.

But then I heard a familiar voice shouting:

"Get your feet *off* the furniture this *instant!*"

Just her voice made my blood boil.

Elle.

I hadn't had to deal with that bitch for what felt like ages but was instantly transported back to when I lived under her "care."

She made Greensward a living hell for me and every other orphan in that place.

Elle didn't care about the kids. She just wanted to profit off the crimes resorted to by the orphans in her care, since she made sure they didn't get any other opportunities.

Just like the fucked-up shit that went down with that scumbag Dominic, when I was forced to steal for that asshole.

I poked my head into the library to see Elle with her nose in a trashy tabloid. Her skin was still orange from her fake tan.

Little kids surrounded her, seeking her attention so they could read to her. But she brushed them all away.

I shook my head in disgust. I was going to take this bitch down.

"Excuse me," I called sweetly.

Elle's bottle blonde head appeared from behind her magazine. When she noticed me, I could practically see her gulp.

That's right, bitch.

"I need to speak with you for a second," I said sweetly.

And then I crossed my arms, waiting for her in the hall.

Our talk would be brief. We wouldn't need to sit.

She came into the hallway and plastered a sickly-sweet smile on her face.

Elle was sucking up to me!

If only my younger self could have seen this.

"Madeline!" she exclaimed. "I wasn't expecting to see *you* here."

I just glared.

"My boyfriends are the ones who donated this building. Loch and Hael Dobrzycka? I'm pretty sure you've heard of them..."

Elle's face fell.

"Boy*friends?*" she asked arrogantly, trying to belittle me.

"Yes, I'm a very lucky girl," I said as I flipped my hair, "and they've assigned me some authority over how this place is run."

Elle was really starting to sweat.

Good.

"It's very important to me that the supervisor of the orphanage has the children's best interests at heart," I explained, "and I know for certain that you do not."

"But—" Elle stammered.

I held my hand up.

"Cut the shit, Elle," I snapped. "When I was in your 'care,' you let Dominic manipulate me into doing illegal shit that could have *totally* fucked up my future. You kicked me out of the only home I had!"

Her eyes were beginning to narrow, the nice act going to shit...

"I want to personally make sure you never do that to another kid again," I said. "You are fucking *fired.*"

Elle stamped her foot.

"Fuck!" she shrieked. "After everything I did for you?"

"Name one thing," I snapped, staring at her blankly. "I'll wait."

"This... This is a hard job, Maddie! You won't find anyone else to do it."

"Oh, please!" I spat. "Get out!"

In what was perhaps the most triumphant moment of my life, I escorted Elle to the front door.

"Sayonara, bitch!" I called, wiping off my hands.

Now that I had taken out the trash, I could focus on other matters.

I headed back through the house and out into the backyard.

Kids swarmed the playground and kicked balls back and forth.

Hael and Loch appeared from a path in the forest. They were followed by a group of children who were all laughing and fighting for their attention.

Oh my God!

I never imagined that my icy mates would be so warm around kids. It was a major turn on.

A young girl tugged on Hael's hand, and he swung her up into his arms.

Awww!

Loch was talking with one of the older boys with spiky hair. He put his arm around the kid's shoulder encouragingly.

AWWWWW!

It was just about all I could handle.

My heart soared as I looked out at the beautiful scene.

The orphanage was shaping up to be the best thing my mates and I had ever done.

ZAYDA

I stared at the ceiling.

After Xythor had died, I went to the nicest department store in Requiem City and spent my internship money on the most luxurious sheets I could buy.

I hoped they might make sleeping easier or even just make me want to go to bed at night.

They did help somewhat, though I still slept on the left side. Xythor always slept on the right.

The night after my fucked-up meeting with Xander, I didn't sleep a wink.

Today I was exhausted. A nap was just what I needed, but I wasn't sure if sleep would come. My mind was racing.

The last place I wanted to be was near Xander again. But he knew just what to say to rope me back in.

If he could bring Xythor back to life, how could I say no?

I closed my eyes and pressed on my eyelids with my fingers.

When I opened them again, my fatigue was so intense that I started to hallucinate...

My ceiling looked different. The edges of the room were rimmed in gold.

I realized then that I was in an entirely different room...

It was another vision.

I was in a luxurious hotel filled with gorgeous baroque furniture and huge mirrors in elaborate frames.

I caught sight of myself in one of them and noticed a figure beside me in the bed.

I whipped my head around and then saw him...

Xythor.

Sleeping peacefully beside me on his stomach.

I would recognize those shoulders anywhere.

I touched the soft skin next to his spine, and he stirred.

He began to turn, and I saw Xythor's face, slack with sleep.

I wanted to call out to him, or scream with delight, but I knew I would just have to enjoy the moment while I had it.

Xythor pulled me under his big arm, and I nestled in close to him.

His body held the same heat it always had.

Running my fingers over his abs, I felt a raised scar.

Xythor had never had that before...

But as I stared up at his face intently, I knew: this was the man I loved. In the flesh.

For the first time since Xythor had died, I felt safe. I felt complete.

I didn't dare close my eyes. I wanted to stay there with him as long as I could.

But eventually, fatigue got the best of me.

Safe in Xythor's arms, I fell asleep...

Later, I woke with a gasp.

I was back in my bedroom, alone, and the sun was setting outside.

I had slept all day...with Xythor.

I laughed out loud. I felt relief so intense that I flopped back into my pillows.

Xythor was coming back. We could be together again.

When I looked at my popcorn ceiling, I thought of the hotel where we were together...

Where we *would be together!* My visions predicted the future, and I could only hope this one was telling me that I'd one day be in his arms again.

That vision was so much better and brighter than my reality, it was all I saw.

As I lay there, my relief slowly combined with a cold dread that settled in my stomach.

I would work with Xander again.

Even though it was the last thing in the world I wanted, anything was worth being with my love again.

MADDIE

Aneurin's hand shot into the stream like a spear. When it emerged, he held a fish.

"Shit!" I cried. "That's awesome!"

"Dragon reflexes," Dane explained.

I sat on the big rock on the bank of the stream. It was damp and cool beneath my legs.

"I'm impressed," I admitted. "You guys have a really cool set-up here."

The twins smiled.

"Thanks, Mads," Aneurin said as he looked around the forest affectionately.

"It sure as hell beats the Quarter," Dane added.

I nodded. It was only by some miracle that we'd all escaped its dark allure.

It warmed my heart that my friends had created a space with all the comforts of a good home.

Especially since I'd known them when they'd had nothing.

Life in the wild clearly suited them. Their skin was tan instead of sickly pale, and they stood straighter and taller.

"You guys look like different people," I said with a smile.

The twins shared a glance.

"We basically are," Dane said.

"Overhead kept us down," Aneurin explained.

"And now you're riding a natural high." I winked.

"Exactly," Dane smirked.

Aneurin eyed the fish in his hand. "You want some dinner, Mads?"

"I have to get home," I told my friends, "but I'll catch you guys later."

After the trek back through the woods, I walked into Req Tower and rode the elevator up to the penthouse.

My mates were in the living room, both holding open books on their laps.

"You guys read?" I asked, leaning in to see the cover of Hael's.

Robinson Crusoe?!

"When we're bored, yes," Loch answered.

"And this is a tremendous tale of adventure," Hael added wistfully before returning to his normal, commandeering tone. "Where have you been, street rat?"

"I was at Dane and Aneurin's campsite. It's actually a really nice space—"

"You know I hate them, mouse," Hael interrupted.

"Well, *I* don't," I shot back, rolling my eyes.

"Watch your attitude. We're the only dragons who get to keep your company." Loch growled possessively and shot me a glare.

So that's what this is about.

Good old-fashioned dragon jealousy.

"Oh, please!" I shouted. "You guys think you're the only dragons that like me?"

My mates stared at me blankly. Their books slipped to the floor.

"Storm *loves* me!" I shouted. "That's why he wants to meet with me all the time. He thinks I'm *powerful.* That I could be the second coming of *Freesia!*"

I finished my big news, thinking it would make my mates laugh.

Or make them *deliciously* mad.

They weren't laughing. They met each other's gazes and then looked back to me.

"Really?" Loch asked.

"Yes!" I replied.

"So, Storm thinks you could be the one to break her curse? So we could leave Requiem?" Hael asked.

I shrugged. It was what *Storm* thought.

The brothers suddenly sprang from the couch and prowled toward me like I was prey.

"This is a very interesting development, indeed, little mouse," Loch smiled.

"We'll help you get to the bottom of this," Hael promised.

I shrugged again.

If I *was* the second coming of this bitch, some backup wouldn't hurt.

CHAPTER 5: SHOT IN THE DARK

ZAYDA

Top floor, a robotic voice said as the elevator went up.

Maddie winked at me through her yellow glasses. They weren't part of the required costume, but they did add a certain edge.

She would be my main competitor. No questions asked.

Harry held up his laser gun and pointed it at Maddie.

"Pew! Pew! Pew!"

"Eat shit, Harry," Maddie snapped.

It had been my idea to play laser tag with the whole crew. And I knew the perfect venue—on top of a skyscraper in downtown Requiem City.

I was ready to blow off some steam with a little exercise.

That morning, I had stopped by Xander's office. I told him I'd do whatever was necessary to bring back my sweet Xythor.

My head knew it was wrong, but my heart didn't have a choice.

I didn't want to think about it anymore.

I was ready to lose myself in a game.

The elevator came to a halt. The doors slid open, and we found ourselves breathing the cold night air. Nets secured the rooftop's wide perimeter, but otherwise it was just us and the open sky. The elevation made adrenaline pump through my veins.

"This is *sick!*" Thea squealed.

Maddie shot Harry in the sensor on his chest.

"Ach!" he cried.

I smiled, feeling the wind whip through my hair.

The course ahead featured raised platforms decorated with fluorescent patterns.

"I can't believe you guys are doing this to me," Darshan pouted as Maddie shot him too.

"We'll be a team." Thea kissed his cheek. "Don't worry, baby. I'll protect you."

That meant those two would spend the whole game making out in a corner. Thea didn't have a competitive bone in her body.

Unlike me.

"First to ten shots is winner!" I shouted.

I dodged Maddie's laser, jumping onto a block and rolling off the other side.

"Dang, Z!" Harry shouted. "You been working out or something?"

If he only fucking knew.

Back on the lowest level, I tracked Maddie as she hopped above.

When I caught a faint motion in the corner of my eye, I knew it was Harry. As he pivoted, I shot him squarely in the chest.

"Oh!"

Got 'im.

Maddie ran toward a distant corner of the roof. She was headed for the lookout point. If she shimmied up the pole to the platform there, she would have the best vantage point on the course.

That was, if she beat *me* there...

I sprinted through the maze, careful to stay in the shadows.

My muscles twitched pleasantly as they drove me forward.

I was gaining on Maddie, and she was oblivious...

Crouched and hidden, I watched her grab the metal pole. When I had the shot, I pulled the trigger.

Maddie's sensor trilled.

"Shit!" she cried, dropping back to the platform. She sunk low on her knees, but I still managed another direct hit.

I stood completely still as she glared out into the darkness.

"Where are you, Zayda?" Maddie demanded in a harsh whisper.

I stood so still that I barely breathed.

I risked another shot, but Maddie dodged it. As she found her footing, she fired right at me. She missed, but my hiding spot was exposed.

I rolled up and over the nearest platform and set off running down a narrow path in the opposite direction.

Green lasers zinged past me as I sprinted.

Maddie was onto me.

She was fast...but not fast enough.

I jumped onto a raised platform and crossed it in two strides before leaping onto the next, higher level.

"Shit!" Maddie screeched below.

When I turned, I saw her contemplating the jump.

We sent a volley of laser blasts at one another, and one of Maddie's hit my sensor.

Fuck.

I turned again, continuing across the platforms to the other corner. Each time I jumped to a new platform, I rose in elevation.

From Maddie's grunts behind me, I knew she had managed the jump as well.

At last, I was at the lookout point on the highest platform of them all.

I pivoted and let my lasers rain down mercilessly on my opponent. Maddie dodged many expertly—though a few met their mark. She was running too quickly to fire back.

The advantage was mine.

But she was gaining on my platform. I kept blasting as she crossed the nearest platform and leapt up to meet me.

As she was in the air, my shot hit its mark.

My vest chirped, alerting me that I'd won the match.

"YES!" I cried, pumping my fist.

"Damn." Maddie moped beside me, but only for a minute. "I gotta give it to you, Z. You're a force to be reckoned with."

I laughed. Maddie always knew just the right words to flatter me.

"Same to you," I replied as we shook hands. "I knew you would be my main competition."

She shrugged, turning to look out at the skyline of Requiem City. We were right at the edge of the building.

The only thing between us and the long way down was a protective net.

The city lights below us were dazzling.

"How you holding up with Xythor and everything?" Maddie asked.

"Oh...you know...okay..." I replied. I wanted to tell Maddie everything. If anyone would understand my predicament, she would.

But I worried even Maddie wouldn't understand what I'd agreed to do.

"Is it nice to have Loch back?" I asked. I often thought of them all together in the penthouse of Req Tower. If I let myself admit it, I was jealous.

Maddie nodded sincerely.

"We opened a new orphanage."

"That's amazing, Maddie," I said sincerely. "I'm glad everything's going so well."

Something shifted in her smile. I knew she was thinking about what a hard time I was having, but there was something else.

"Thanks, Z. But it's not all flowers and butterflies." She paused.

"There's been some weird stuff, too. Do you know Storm?"

"Kind of," I replied. I remembered the mysterious man from Xythor's funeral.

"He's a dragon," she explained, rolling her eyes. "He keeps telling me...troubling things."

"Oh," I replied. My heartbeat quickened. I was suddenly curious.

Just then, a beam of white light shot up from the center of the course.

"Everyone come here!" Darshan's voice called from a loudspeaker.

"Sounds like we're being summoned," Maddie chuckled. I climbed down into the dark space and helped Maddie down.

We headed toward the light. I wanted to press her for more information about this Storm guy, but we didn't have much time.

"Have you still been seeing Xander?" Maddie asked.

"Not really," I replied. But I saw in Maddie's eyes genuine concern.

It would feel good to be honest.

"Well...yeah. I have. And he gave me some troubling news too."

She sighed angrily, igniting a fire within me.

"I didn't exactly go see him of my own volition," I shot back, shaking my head. I should've known Maddie would judge me.

"Why can't you just cut him off?" she asked seriously.

"It's a little...complicated," I managed.

How could I tell Maddie what I'd decided?

She stared at me with concern in her eyes...and fear.

As we reached our friends, the conversation concluded, leaving us both with more questions than answers.

"*There* you guys are," Harry cried.

"Okay, finally," Darshan called. "I wanted to make an announcement in front of my closest and oldest friends."

"Awww!" Maddie shouted ironically.

Darshan smirked.

"You all know I'm obsessed with Thea," Darshan began.

Thea flipped her hair, loving the attention.

"And I want to take the next step..."

With that, Darshan got down on one knee and held Thea's hand.

O-M-G!

I covered my mouth. We all gasped.

"Thea, I've never seen you, but somehow I know for sure that you're the most beautiful woman in the world..."

Thea began to cry, and tears pricked my own eyes.

"All I want to do is be with you...forever..." Darshan kissed our friend's hand. She gazed down at him lovingly, overcome with emotion.

"Thea, will you marry me?"

MADDIE

"Who else wants wine?" I called out from the kitchen. Hael and Loch were in the living room when I stumbled into the penthouse.

To celebrate Thea and Darshan's engagement, we'd headed for the closest bar and drank accordingly.

Now, I filled my glass to the brim with some priceless vintage from the Dobrzyckas' wine cabinet. Having billionaire mates certainly had *some* advantages.

"None for me," Loch replied.

"Rat, could you get me some cow blood?" Hael asked.

I strode into the living room and plopped down on the couch between my mates.

"No."

I took a swig.

"In a bad mood, mouse?" Loch asked.

I considered the question.

Am I?

My conversation with Zayda left me feeling...weird. And as

happy as I was for Thea and Darshan, I had to admit I was feeling something else.

Jealousy.

"No," I pouted. "I'm celebrating. Thea and Darshan got engaged."

"Isn't that cute," Hael teased.

I sat up, sloshing wine onto my leg.

"Yes, it is cute," I replied, glaring daggers at Hael. "And romantic. And sweet. And normal. But I guess you guys wouldn't know anything about that."

My mates met each other's gazes and raised their eyebrows.

"Watch it, mouse," Loch warned.

"You want to marry us, rat?" Hael sneered.

I glared at him once more. Hael was pushing my buttons on purpose. Why I ever thought he was the nicer brother was a mystery to me.

"No, I do not," I spat. "I want a relationship that is even *slightly* normal. Where my partners are 'boyfriends,' not 'mates,' and I don't have a fucking *brand* that ties me to them against my will!"

My rant hung in the air a moment as I took another sloppy sip. I was feeling moody as hell.

My words were *mostly* true. Maybe some part of me *did* want to marry them. The brand wasn't the only thing that tied us together.

I knew in my heart that even without that physical mark, I would still be here. Loch and Hael would still be my mates.

We cared for each other—even if we had a fucked-up way of showing it.

"Against your will?" Loch asked with a smirk.

"You're pushing it, mouse. Want us to lock you in your cage again?" Hael glared at me.

That was the last straw. My drunkenness overpowered my sentimental thoughts, and I rocketed upward, spilling red wine everywhere.

"No fucking way!" I shouted. "You *snakes* will never lock me up *again!*"

With that, I turned on my heel and charged down the hallway, not caring about the wine trail I left behind.

I wished Loch and Hael would follow me, or at least call after me, but they didn't.

I passed the master bedroom and continued to the space I'd adopted as a dressing room.

I slammed the door behind me and sat in front of my vanity.

In the mirror, I saw my teeth stained red from the wine.

I let my head fall into my hands.

Hael's threat made my old fear fresh again. In that moment, I hated the way they made me feel.

I hated how I had felt, locked in that cage back when our relationship had first begun.

I had felt so helpless to the power of our mate bond. It... was it... love? Love... it held a sway over you, no matter your intention, no matter how hard you wanted to have a choice. When I let that stupid feeling consume me, in those moments, I was tethered to them completely and all my fight slipped away.

I hated that fated feeling of overwhelming vulnerability.

I couldn't let myself be too open with dragon lords—they'd take advantage of it in a heartbeat. I was sure of it.

But as the minutes passed, I got sick of being angry.

I was drunk and lonely. I wanted to see my mates, but I didn't want to swallow my pride.

I stared at myself in the mirror. My thoughts were all over the place.

With my smudged mascara, I looked like a mess.

I wished that Hael or Loch would come get me, but why would they? I had just blown up at them basically for no reason. I'd gone from brat to super brat.

But fuck. They would never get me. I just wanted to be *normal.* Was that too much to ask?

I didn't want to uncover my family's history for some evil dragon. I didn't want to worry that the men I loved would lock me in a cage if I disobeyed them. Or simply if they got into a particularly shitty mood.

I sighed, dropping my head into my hands.

Well, it's not like I'm in a cage now.

I knew I could walk out of the penthouse for good if I wanted.

But I didn't want to...

Suddenly, I realized that I couldn't blame Loch and Hael for all of this. Staying with them was my choice.

I was stuck in the cage of love.

When I confronted my reflection once more, my red hair fell around my face.

I was a mess. And I had no idea where to turn for help.

Maybe that feeling of loneliness was an absence, something was missing. Maybe it was my talk with Storm, which was still ringing in my ears...

I wondered if I looked like my mother.

What was she like, the woman who had birthed me?

What would she say if she could see me now?

CHAPTER 6: GARDEN EXPERT

MADDIE

"Miss Maddie?" a little, high-pitched voice called, "what's *this* flower?"

I turned to find Angeline, AKA my biggest fan, smiling up at me.

"That is a pink flower...with yellow dots on it," I replied, flashing her a smile.

Okay, so I wasn't exactly a nature expert. But I was still leading the garden tour through the grounds of the Dobrzycka mansion, so I had to give her something.

Angeline's eyes widened with wonder. She smiled her adorable, gap-toothed smile.

"Wow!" she whispered.

The kids in my nature explorers group climbed over the benches in the gazebo.

While many of the children preferred to entertain themselves, Angeline stood by my side.

At six years old, she stood as tall as my thigh. She was rail thin and had freckles across her cheeks and arms.

Because she was an orphan, she reminded me of myself at her age.

But where I was scrappy and spunky, Angeline was tender and sweet.

"For you, Miss Maddie," Angeline said, tugging on my denim shorts. When I looked down, she was hiding her blushing face behind a pink flower.

I beamed at my favorite little orphan.

"Cowabunga!!" A boy's voice tore through my thoughts.

"Jimmy! Out of the dirt!" I shouted.

The little boy had jumped from the railing of the gazebo into the flower beds.

Jimmy was a reliable troublemaker.

Maybe I had been more like him when I was a kid...

I felt a tap on my shoulder and turned to find Adara standing behind me. She wore a sleek legging and sports bra combo, and her hair was slicked back in a ponytail.

She looked like a celebrity personal trainer, not the gym teacher at an orphanage.

"Time for gymnastics with Miss Adara!" I told the kids.

The girls shrieked with delight. The boys groaned.

Adara blew the golden whistle that hung around her neck and beckoned the children to follow her. Angeline hesitated by my side.

I crouched so I was at her eye level. "Ready to follow your friends?" I asked.

Angeline looked at her feet. She wore dirty pink and white Velcro sneakers that lit up with each step.

She shook her head.

"Could I sit with you, Miss Maddie?" she asked, still not meeting my eye.

"Of course," I took her little hand in mine and led her toward the mansion.

We passed through the lush gardens along a winding path. To our left, the enormous playscape loomed over us.

I took a seat on the back steps leading to the house and pulled Angeline onto my lap.

"You don't want to play?" I asked.

Angeline didn't reply. She just began to touch the mint bracelet on my wrist.

"What's this?" she asked.

"Uh..."

How could I explain? I was struck once more by the bizarre circumstances of my relationship.

Angeline was so young and innocent. As she sat on my lap, I felt old. Hardened to the world.

And it made me sad.

It wasn't like I was mourning the loss of my innocence. I was pretty sure I had never had any to begin with.

But as I held Angeline on my lap, I was overcome with the desire to protect her. I wanted to make sure she never went through what I had.

I didn't want her to hustle on the streets. I didn't want her to fight for her freedom in relationships with the people or dragons she loved.

Angeline looked up at me expectantly.

"It's my special bracelet," I finally replied.

It was better than: "It keeps my domineering dragon mates from reading my mind and controlling me more than they already do."

My bracelet was tied to much of my inner conflict, but I couldn't explain that to a child. I could hardly explain it to myself.

I wanted love but didn't want to be controlled. But was that possible, even if my mates *weren't* domineering dragons?

I didn't want to need Hael and Loch so badly because it meant that they were able to control me.

But I was starting to realize that needing someone came along with loving them. And that meant that love was always tied to control.

I sighed, returning to the world after spacing out.

Angeline was still inspecting my wrist, touching the center bead where the liquid mint was kept.

"I like your special bracelet," she said.

"Thanks, Angeline."

Though it was silly, my little buddy's approval made me feel somewhat better.

I didn't have everything figured out by any means. But even though my life confused me, I knew I was lucky.

"Let's go inside, huh?" I asked her.

She stood and reached for my hand. We entered the orphanage through the back door. I heard Loch's and Hael's voices coming from the library.

When we reached the doorway, I peered in to watch them.

My mates were sitting on a couch. Before them was a handful of older kids who huddled around two boys playing a board game.

"Are you playing chess?" I asked.

Hael turned to me and winked. "Hey, mouse. Something like that."

"Dragon chess!" the kid with knotty hair cried. "The hardest strategy game in the whole *world*."

I lowered my eyes at my mates. What were they up to?

They both smiled at me innocently before returning their attention to the board.

I stepped closer and found that the board itself was made of ivory and dark wood. It was checkered like a chess board, and intricate swirls laced the whole surface.

The pieces were made of gold. Each one was a unique, abstract shape.

I couldn't take my eyes off of the beautiful game. Something about it entranced me.

When I looked up, I saw my mates staring at a spiky-haired boy named Zak.

There was something strange about this scene.

What did they have up their sleeves? What kind of game were they really playing?

ZAYDA

I held the lavender up to my nose, inhaling the calming scent.

I snipped some stalks and placed them in my bag.

After following my nose through the forest, my bag was full of herbs.

When I had woken up that morning, hungover and anxious, I'd headed to the forest to soothe my mind. My plan was to create a soothing tonic with the herbs I foraged.

The collection of calming plants relaxed me. At least, somewhat.

Celebrating Darshan and Thea's engagement was just the break from reality that I'd needed.

But even when I got drunk enough to forget my troubles, I still felt something off between me and Maddie. Like we needed to have another talk that neither of us were ready for.

When I woke up with a pounding headache and a nauseous stomach, all my problems came rushing back. My exchange with Maddie made me realize just what I was getting myself into.

It was Saturday, and on Monday I would return to Xander's lab. Just the thought of returning to XU made me sick.

Especially because I knew what I needed to do...

When Xander had needed my help in the past, it was because I was a star student and a powerful mage. I put in hard work at the lab and was an asset to his team.

But this time would be different.

My role in resurrecting Xythor required no skill. I hardly even had to step foot in the lab.

I just had to give my blood.

Part of me was relieved because I wouldn't have to spend as much time with Xander. The other part was revolted that I was letting my body be used this way.

I knew Xander was untrustworthy but was trusting him once again.

I knew he was powerful but was giving him power over me.

When Xythor's here, it will all be worth it. I won't even have to think about what I did to bring him back.

I tried to steady my breathing but was full-on panicking. Anxiety bubbled up inside me.

I stuffed my head back into my bag, inhaling the lavender, marjoram, and birch bark...

I needed to make my soothing tonic stat. I was a mess.

Such a mess that my head spun... I fell onto the forest floor and felt the dead leaves press into my bare skin.

Though the herbs relieved me, I was overcome by a wave of nausea.

I gagged and threw up onto the ground.

I opened my watering eyes.

What was going on with me?

Everything felt wrong.

One moment, my body was bursting with unbridled strength. The next, I was on the ground vomiting.

I swallowed the bile that threatened to rise again.

But then I had a terrifying thought:

What if what happened to Xythor was happening to me?

CHAPTER 7: FUN AT DUSK

MADDIE

I stared up into the trees. All I could say was, "Wow."

"Pretty cool, huh?" Aneurin asked with his hands on his hips.

Of the new changes to Dane and Aneurin's forest abode that I had seen so far, my favorite was their bedroom.

Well, the place where they slept in the trees.

They had added a wooden platform, like a treehouse, with a couch and some chairs.

Their new hammocks stretched between far away trunks. The fabrics were deep colors and looked delicate as silk.

Of course, I couldn't help but notice that there were more than two.

"Did you guys find out you have more brothers or something?" I asked.

Dane chuckled. "Nah. But it's nice to sleep in different places. I guess that's something we got used to in the Quarter."

"And we wanted to have a place for people to crash if they want," Aneurin elaborated. "We're not exactly central out here."

I nodded. That was true. I'd trekked through the forest for an hour to get here.

"There's another thing that we found..." Dane said, smiling mischievously.

The brothers practically skipped, they were so excited. We headed through the dense trees until a rock ledge rose above us.

Aneurin waved me over toward a cave in the rock face.

I peered into it, but dusk was falling, and I couldn't see much. I turned on the flashlight on my phone...

"*NO*," I gasped.

Before me was a genuine treasure trove. I had only seen something like it at Loch and Hael's.

"You guys *found* this?!" I demanded.

The floor of the sizable cavern was carpeted in a thick layer of gold coins. In the center, a larger than life diamond sparkled as if it were lit from within.

"Could I—?" I asked as I headed into the cave.

"Easy, tiger," Aneurin called. "Nothing leaves the cave...for now. We don't know who it belongs to, so we're watching over it for a while."

I scowled but nodded.

"Alright, then get me away from here, please."

My friends guided me back through the woods. When we reached the clearing, Dane sprinted to the other side.

"Check this out, Mads!"

Black mist covered his feet, and he shifted into a dragon before my eyes.

The transition was smooth and fast. I was stunned at the progress he'd made. Just a few weeks ago, such a transformation would've seemed impossible.

I watched the black dragon push off his strong back legs and shoot up into the sky like a bullet.

When Dane reached the treetops, he reversed directions and dove back down. Just as he was about to hit the ground, he opened his wings at the last moment and soared toward Aneurin and me.

"We're getting pretty good," Aneurin smirked.

"No, kidding!" I cried. My mouth was hanging open.

"Why don't you—?" I began, but he was already misting.

He reappeared in his dragon form, mid-flight, rocketing after his brother.

Dane's scales were jet black with an iridescent sheen, while Aneurin's were a pure and shining gold.

I cheered as Aneurin followed Dane, and they angled gracefully up into the dusky sky.

I could hardly believe that merely a month ago, these two didn't know they were dragons.

Their football was lying in the grass, so I scooped it up and hid it behind my back.

The brothers landed as if they were light as feathers. They misted back to their human forms.

I whooped and clapped.

"Hey! Think fast!" I launched the football at them. Dane caught it effortlessly then threw it back.

As I ran for it, I felt my foot catch on a stray root and fell on my knee. Hard. I looked down at the scrape on my leg. I was bleeding, and the skin had rubbed off. It stung like a bitch, but I was determined to walk it off.

"That's a bad scrape, Maddie," Aneurin said with a wince.

The brothers met each other's eyes and nodded.

"There's one more new addition we have to show you, Mads," Dane said.

"It's gonna help you, tough guy," Aneurin promised, punching my arm.

"What, you guys have a first-aid tent out here now?" I teased.

They didn't reply.

Together, we followed the stream, and when it broke in two, we stayed to the left.

Our fork led to a round pool that glimmered faintly green in the fading light.

"Wow," I whispered. It was beautiful, and I couldn't look away. As a current swirled up from the deep, the water bubbled gently.

"Put your legs in," Dane ordered.

I narrowed my eyes at him.

"There aren't piranhas in here, are there?" I asked. But really, I had a feeling that the water was safe. It enticed me, drawing me forward.

I flung off my sneakers and sat at the edge of the pool.

As my skin touched the water, I gasped. The pool felt warm and calm, and my scrape tingled pleasantly.

A moment later, I withdrew my injured leg only to find that the skin had healed completely.

"What the heck?!"

"It's a healing pond," Aneurin grinned. "Another awesome feature of our new digs."

I nodded. "Pretty sick."

We stayed for a while like that, gazing into the water. I kept my feet inside, feeling my whole body warmed by the pool.

"Want a ride back to Req Tower, Maddie?" Dane asked finally. "I want to stretch my wings anyway."

"I think I'll wait here a little longer, if that's okay."

My mates would be leaving the orphanage soon, and I didn't really want to arrive home before them. I was worried I'd get moody and mope in front of the mirror again.

The brothers said goodbye, and I watched them take off and fly up through the trees.

When I was alone, I leaned back onto the forest floor.

I stared up into the canopy above me as darkness continued to fall.

I could stay here all night, I thought to myself.

I felt so comfortable here by the water. And around Dane and Aneurin in general.

Their outdoor abode was so freeing. By contrast, my home at Req Tower felt restrictive.

Even though I wasn't living in the golden cage, I couldn't help but wonder what it would be like to live out here in the wild...

Hael and Loch were such city boys. I couldn't imagine them roughing it in the wilderness. But they *were* reading adventure novels the other night...

I let my eyes close and my thoughts wander.

I pulled my legs from the water. Suddenly, I felt like I was falling down a hole.

The sensation was familiar at this point.

Not again!

But it had already begun.

I was having a vision.

My sight blurred at the edges as I gazed out into the night.

A woman was weeping.

The red-haired woman who I had come to know...

Freesia.

She wore a long, ragged dress that was of another time.

From above, I gazed down at her quaking figure.

On her knees, she pounded her fists on the ground.

She crawled forward, pulling herself over the grass toward a red rock that was stuck through in one spot with a handful of swords.

The rock was jagged and massive.

She slammed her hand against it.

Was she trying to hurt herself?

As her hand slowly left the rock, it left behind a slick trail of bright red blood.

The flow of blood only increased as her hand passed over the rock's surface...

As if the rock itself was bleeding.

The scene before me faded to black...

And another materialized...

I was in a small academic office, peering down from above.

When I could make out the faces before me, my stomach recoiled.

Xander.

He was younger, his hair bright red and curly. But youth did nothing to soften his features.

"How is Serena taking to the treatments?" asked the man sitting across Xander's desk. He appeared to be another professor. His pipe sent smoke curling to the ceiling.

"Not well," Xander replied. His thin lips moved like worms. "But according to plan."

"Poor woman," his colleague said, chuckling harshly.

These men revolted me. Who was Serena? What had they done to her?

"She suffers, but for a noble task," Xander replied, his voice rising with excitement.

He paused a moment.

"I wonder, when the child is born, if the rock will bleed..."

My blood ran ice cold. What child?

"It is possible," his colleague mused. "There is great potential..."

Xander, the monster who was my father, smiled a twisted smile.

"The child will be useful," Xander replied. "Very useful, indeed."

I woke with a start, pushing myself up to sitting.

What the fuck was that?

I'd had some fucked-up visions.

But this was on a whole other level.

Around me, darkness had fallen. The only light beneath the dense canopy came from the healing pool, which seemed to glow more brightly than before.

A sour smell rose from my armpits. Fear.

I crawled to the edge of the pool and put my hand into the water.

Immediately, my anxiety lessened. I drew in a long, steady breath.

Night had fallen, and the deep woods around me chirped with insects.

I didn't even know what time it was.

Once I felt like my health was restored, I pulled out my phone.

It was exactly midnight.

The witching hour.

It was more than a little freaky. But I brushed it off. Loch and Hael were probably getting worried about me.

Turning on the flashlight on my phone, I set off back to Dane and Aneurin's campsite. I hoped it wasn't too late to accept their offer for a ride home.

ZAYDA

I gazed up at the Xander University sign.

When I first began school here, I had thought it looked regal.

Now, it nearly made me sick.

I sighed and took a long drink from my water bottle.

It was Monday morning. The first day of my secret life.

I didn't even tell my roommates what I was up to. Not that Thea and Darshan were ever around. They'd basically been on a honeymoon since they'd gotten engaged.

I watched the other students bustling on the sidewalks or stopping to share the weekend gossip outside the old, stone buildings.

Once, I'd been a student like them. But after Maddie and the rest of my friends were expelled, people looked at me funny.

Now, I knew that word had gotten out that Xythor was a dragon.

At a dragon slayers' school, it didn't exactly win me Miss Popularity.

I took a deep breath, summoning Xythor's optimism.

I was here to save him. To bring him back. For that, I would do anything.

I stepped onto the campus and started toward the lab, trying to avoid everyone's gaze.

Keeping my eyes on the ground, I walked my solitary path.

Suddenly, a scream broke through my focus.

It was coming from the chapel that held Freesia's Rock...

I sprinted toward the small chapel, determined to see what was wrong. The mahogany doors were blocked with warning signs and flimsy barriers.

DANGER ZONE: BEWARE OF BLOOD

I pushed past them. When I was inside the dim building, I saw the screaming girl.

She held her hand as if she was wounded. But then students crowded around her, and I couldn't make out what was wrong.

I pushed my way through. And then I saw the rock. Swords protruded from a point on top of the massive rock. Oddly, blood seemed to be dribbling down its sharp side.

The sight and the screams chilled me to my core.

"The burn is bad," a student cried from over the girl's shoulder. I recognized him from one of my old potion classes. "The skin's all gone."

I leaned closer and finally glimpsed her hand. Her flesh was red and raw, and the air smelled like overcooked meat.

"We have to take her to the medical center!" I cried.

As I moved to help her, I felt a firm grip on my shoulder. I turned to see the hateful face of an old classmate.

"Move, dragon-fucker," he spat, pushing me out of the way.

CHAPTER 8: ZAYDA'S DUTIES

ZAYDA

I hustled through the paths of Xander University with my head down. I moved like a ghost, hoping to escape the eyes of my peers. Since the incident earlier, when I was pushed, I could no longer deny how the other students felt about me.

The tension that bubbled beneath my peers' steely expressions rose to the surface.

Everyone knew about my relationship with Xythor, and nobody cared about my pain.

I was a dragon-lover at a school of dragon slayers. And they hated me.

I walked to Xander's lab. It felt like I was heading to prison.

This was my sentence. My punishment for the crime of love.

Xander was waiting for me when I arrived.

He didn't say much or pretend that we would be happy to see each other.

It was straight to business.

"The rock is bleeding," he told me, his voice grave.

"What does it mean?" I asked.

"It means our work is all the more important."

I searched his stern expression but found no clues. If I wanted to know why the stone bled, I'd need to look elsewhere.

Not wasting any time, we began the blood work.

I followed Xander into a room where he'd drawn my blood a few times before. I'd lain on the gurney many times before, but this time felt different than our Blood Raven experiments.

Xander's voice seemed to come from far away when he told me he'd be taking twelve fluid ounces. Twelve ounces today, and every day I went to the lab afterward.

Since I was a Blood Raven, my body could handle the rigorous schedule.

I shut my eyes as the needle went into my arm and didn't open them until it was over.

"That's enough work for today," Xander said.

His dismissal communicated to me the truth: that I never had any talent. I wasn't a gifted mage. My only worth came from my body. Specifically from my blood.

I walked home lightheaded, but the sight of the pink sunset overhead revitalized me. I felt truly hopeful for the first time since Xythor's death.

Today, I'd taken the first step to getting my soulmate back.

Soon, everything would be okay.

XANDER

"Good evening, Zayda," I said, greeting Zayda as she walked in for our second session the following day.

"Evening," she replied, dropping herself onto a seat. She didn't meet my eyes.

I could tell she was upset. It was unfortunate to see her in such a weak condition, but I knew my plan could only work if she were desperate.

"Did you notice the rock? The bleeding has increased," I informed her.

Her body stiffened.

"No, I didn't," she replied.

Zayda didn't understand the complexity of Freesia's Rock, but she intuited its significance.

I was the only one who knew it all.

It was common knowledge that the rock bled because of Freesia's Curse. But few remembered that the curse was tiered, and each tier was stained with a different blood.

When Freesia sacrificed her own child, she had scattered its blood around the borders of Requiem City, binding those demonic dragons to our land.

Because of her sacrifice, the beasts could no longer terrorize the world at large.

After the death of their child, Freesia's mates fought each other to the end.

To escape certain death, Freesia used magic to break their mateship bond and join with her fellow mages.

They raged against the dragons of Requiem City together. In the gruesome battle, Freesia and the mages killed all the Twin Leading Breeds of the city.

And they bled them into the rock.

Freesia's Rock.

And now the rock was bleeding once more.

It meant that war was coming to Requiem. Humans and dragons would wage their bloody battle for the land again.

Something was shifting in the dragons of Requiem.

The beasts might not know it yet themselves, but their ancestors felt it.

The blood of those ancient beasts was boiling deep within the stone, leaking into our world from the hell pit where they burned.

The fate of Requiem City would fall into the hands of the dragon slayers.

I needed to build an army to protect the good people of this city. To stomp out the dragon threat once and for all.

Zayda didn't know this. She couldn't.

The dragon sympathizer was unreliable, but useful nevertheless. She would help my cause, and in return, I'd give her what I had promised.

I was harvesting Zayda's blood so that she could have her scaly lover back again.

But that wasn't all.

Not by a long shot.

"Alright, then," I said. "It's time for your daily blood work."

ZAYDA

After the procedure, I dragged my feet down the halls.

Just like the day before, my strength fell after the bloodwork.

But at least I could leave the lab now that it was over.

While my days as an intern had been long, now they only took as long as the harvest required. This was the one saving grace.

"One more thing, Zayda!" Xander called from behind me.

Ugh. What else could this leech possibly want from me?

I turned and slowly trudged back to the lab.

"Yes?" I asked. My tone was flat and unfeeling.

"I have a task to be completed by our evening session tomorrow night."

I nodded, staring into space. He held out a small vial.

"Please fill this with blood from Freesia's Rock. This will be a crucial ingredient in the next phase of our little resurrection."

The request cut through the fog in my mind.

I met Xander's eyes.

"But the blood is dangerous," I protested, thinking of the girl's burned hand.

"Then be careful," he said, his voice calm.

I swallowed, staring into his dark, unfeeling eyes.

"Okay," I replied through tight lips. I took the vial and left the lab.

As I walked the hallway once more, adrenaline cut through my fatigue.

I emerged onto campus to find it empty. It was late at night.

I stalked the pathways that led me to the chapel. I opened the mahogany door and soon found myself standing before the rock. A small lamp illuminated the plaque beside it, which honored Freesia's sacrifice.

These dragon slayers were obsessed with the baby killer.

I eyed the rock uneasily. Blood trickled down its craggy surface.

Xander was right. The flow had increased since yesterday.

It dripped to the ground in one fat rivulet.

I held my vial in a shaking hand and moved toward the rock.

I crouched before it, careful to avoid where the blood pooled on the floor.

As I stretched toward the stream trickling from the rock, I lost my balance. My hand came down to catch me...

Directly in the puddle.

I muffled a scream and pulled my hand out of the sticky substance. I braced myself, waiting for the burning to begin.

But, strangely, it didn't come.

My hand was covered in blood, but it was only warm. I didn't burn.

I looked at the rich, red liquid that dripped down my hand.

Why did it burn the other student, but leave me unscathed?

Could it mean that Xander was right?

Was I the second coming of Freesia?

When I got home to the apartment, Thea was sitting on our living room floor surrounded by wedding magazines.

"Zaydaaa," she groaned.

"Hey, girl," I said, plopping down beside her, my spirits buoyed by the unexpected presence of my friend. "Where's Darshan?"

"I sent him home so I could think clearly about the wedding," Thea explained. "Turns out, these things are hard as *fuck* to plan."

"I'll help you," I said, touching her arm.

She gave me a relieved smile.

I picked up a magazine. This was exactly what I needed to take my mind off of my own fucked-up life.

Inside, I saw skinny, pretty women in white dresses.

What would it be like to feel like this? I wondered.

To be normal?

Thea sighed dramatically.

My friend didn't know how lucky she was.

"I definitely want to get married outside," Thea mused. "Maybe on a farm. And we need a live band."

What would it be like if planning a wedding was my only concern?

"Darshan said he'll take care of the food..." Thea went on.

"It's going to be beautiful, T."

We met each other's eyes and smiled.

"I think I'd like a drink," Thea decided, getting to her feet. "I have some leftover margarita mix. They're apple cinnamon flavored. My favorite! Want one?"

Thinking about the nasty booze Thea liked always made me feel sick, but now I felt like I might *actually* throw up.

Oh, boy.

I was going to be sick. Again.

I stood up and sprinted to the bathroom. I didn't even have time to close the door behind me as I wretched into the toilet.

"Oh my God!" Thea cried from the doorway.

I lay my cheek against the cool porcelain. Thea crouched next to me and rubbed my back.

"Are you sick, Zayda?" she asked in a soft voice.

"I don't know," I replied.

Thea considered this as she continued to scratch soothing circles on my back.

"Oh my God!" she shrieked. "Are you pregnant?"

My heart dropped.

"No way," I said.

But then I suddenly got worried.

Xythor and I had used protection...most of the time. And he was a dragon. Could dragons even make people pregnant?

I gulped as the realization hit home...

Yes.

Freesia was a Blood Raven impregnated by Twin Leading Breeds. I was a Blood Raven too. If she could have a dragon baby, I could too.

"I have a test," Thea shouted, running to her room and returning with a stick in a plastic wrapper.

I pulled out the test.

"Want me to give you a minute?" Thea asked as I tugged down my pants.

"Definitely not," I replied. I needed a friend now more than ever, no matter what the test said.

I shut my eyes. After a full minute of concentration and Thea's encouragement, I was finally able to pee on the stick.

When I looked at the little window three tense minutes later, my heart stopped.

Positive.

My mind was a blank slate. I was emotionless with shock.

I was pregnant.

Thea's hand was steady on my shoulder.

She grounded me as I willed myself to breathe.

I appreciated that she wasn't freaking out. She was being strong for me.

"It's gonna be okay, Zayda," she assured me.

I nodded. I willed my mind to think, but it was stuck.

"Have you... Since Xythor?" she asked.

I shook my head.

She squeezed my arm.

All at once, my brain kicked into motion and went spinning in one hundred frenzied directions.

My nightmarish life had just gotten darker. I wasn't just alone.

I was *pregnant* and all alone.

CHAPTER 9: GIRL TALK GONE WRONG

MADDIE

I strolled onto the terrace at the rooftop bar five minutes after our planned meeting time. Zayda was already there. *Classic goody two-shoes.*

I scolded myself for my bratty attitude. I knew Zayda was hurting right now and just wanted a friend.

When she texted me this morning to meet up, I'd immediately agreed.

But the more I thought about the last time we had talked, at laser tag, I got frustrated.

How could I help her if she couldn't help herself?

She'd suggested that she was still working for Xander. If that was true, I didn't want anything to do with her.

Since my disturbing vision, my hatred for Xander had only grown. I was thinking about him a lot, and I knew I would have to speak to him sooner or later.

I wanted answers. And he was the only one who had them.

And once I had what I wanted, I would cut my father out of my life for good.

"Hey, Zayda," I called as I slid into the seat beside her.

"Hey," she smiled. But I could tell she was nervous. "Thanks for meeting."

"Of course. I'm looking forward to catching up."

That much was true. I was excited to hear what was really going on with Zayda.

When a waiter appeared at the table, I ordered a martini without looking at the menu. Zayda ordered a lemonade.

"My stomach has been feeling a little strange today," she explained.

I shrugged. It never bothered me to be the only one drinking.

We watched the waitress walk away and then return with our drinks. Mine was strong and briny, like seawater.

"So, what's up?" I asked.

She took a deep breath.

Sheesh! Why is this girl so nervous?

"I wanted to catch up in general, of course. And I wanted to hear about the meeting with Storm that you mentioned."

Zayda gave me a little smile.

"Oh, that," I said, waving my hand. "Of course. And I want to hear about what you mentioned, too. About Xander."

"Totally," she said too quickly. "You want to go first?"

I took a long drink. "Definitely."

I reflected back on what Storm had said. Just the memory made my vodka-tipsy mind go red with anger.

"First of all, *fuck* Storm!" I cried.

Zayda leaned her elbows onto the table, ready for the gossip.

"So you know how Loch was in a murderous rage? When he was Lochness or whatever?" I asked, rolling my eyes.

Zayda nodded intently.

"Well, it turns out that was all *Storm's fault!* He placed a rage charm on Loch!"

Zayda gasped. "*No.*"

"Yes!" I snapped. "He did it to test me. How fucked is *that?*

Apparently, I'm really powerful or something."

I flipped my hair over my shoulder and finished off my martini. "And he wanted to see if I could save Loch."

"Well, you did," Zayda said with a smirk.

"Yeah, I did."

I smiled. I didn't mean to brag, but it felt good.

Of course, I also remembered what Storm had said about Zayda. That my friend was powerful too. But could she really be stronger than *me?*

If she was, I certainly didn't want her knowing it.

"Storm said that to find out just what I'm capable of, I need to learn more about my birth parents. My mom in particular," I said with a sigh.

Zayda nodded understandingly.

"I don't want to," I continued, "but apparently it's important..."

I met her gaze before I delivered the final blow.

"Because Storm thinks I'm the second coming of Freesia."

ZAYDA

My mouth hung open. I couldn't help it.

"But...Xander says that *I* might be the second coming of Freesia!"

"What?!" Maddie practically shouted. If she hadn't finished her martini, she would have spat it out.

"I mean, fuck Xander too. I can't even get started on that," I went on. "But it kinda makes sense since now I'm apparently a dragon *and* a blood mage."

I broke into an exasperated smile.

All of this was *so crazy.*

But when I looked back at Maddie, she wasn't smiling.

In fact, she looked pissed.

"Xander's just manipulating you," Maddie scoffed. "He wants

you to think you're powerful to make you feel better about killing Xythor."

My jaw dropped all over again.

I always knew Maddie had a big mouth, but this was next level.

"*Excuse me?*" I demanded.

Maddie just stared at me with that stupid smirk on her face.

"Look," I hissed. "I *am* powerful, Maddie, whether I like it or not. And being the second coming of that *killer* would not make me feel better about losing Xythor."

Maddie stood up. "Don't talk about Freesia like that," she shouted.

What the fuck?

Was my friend brainwashed?

"You wouldn't be able to handle it anyway," Maddie added.

"Handle *what?*" I asked, exasperated.

"*The pressure,*" she hissed.

"I don't *want* it, Maddie," I yelled.

With that, Maddie stormed out of the bar.

It was only then that I realized: Maddie *did* want it. Even if she wouldn't admit it.

Maddie felt threatened that I might be the second coming of Freesia instead of her.

The whole thing was so crazy it made my head spin.

Our get-together had been a total disaster, and I hadn't even gotten to tell her that I was pregnant. Or that I was bringing Xythor back from the dead.

I sighed, dropping my head into my hands.

Would we *ever* have a normal friendship?

LOCH

"Nicely done," I congratulated Zak, clapping him heartily on the back.

Hael met my eye and winked.

Zak smiled down at the game board before him. His little opponent sulked with his arms crossed over his chest.

The other boys in the library crowded around, excitedly discussing Zak's victory.

Hael: You know what this means, brother.

Hael: He passed the test.

Loch: Let's congratulate our newest recruit.

I smiled at my brother. It was true—Zak had passed the test with flying colors. The game of dragon's chess worked on two levels.

Like the simplified, human version of the game, it required strategy and intuition. And Zak had outwitted his opponent.

The other boy had shown promise as well, but now it was clear that Zak was superior. And while the players reacted to the game, the game responded to the players.

I watched the gold pieces that Zak touched glow a soft red. That would be the color of his dragon. When he'd been trained enough to shift. Of course, the glow could only be seen by other dragons. That was why Hael and I used it in our little recruiting endeavor.

"Mind if my brother and I borrow you for a minute?" Hael asked.

Zak nodded, and we all stood up.

I felt the eyes of the other children on our backs. Their jealousy was obvious. And if they knew what we were really up to, their jealousy would go through the roof.

When we were out in the garden, I began my speech.

"Great job in there, Zak," I said with a fraternal smile. "It's not often that we see young people with so much promise."

He shrugged. "It's a fun game."

Hael grinned. "It sure is. And it gets even better. That's what my brother and I want to talk to you about."

"I wanted to talk with you, too," Zak replied. "I appreciate all you guys have done for me, but I've decided I'm going to leave the orphanage."

"What?!" I demanded.

Hael's eyes burned.

"You ungrateful piece of—" my brother hissed under his breath before I shot him a warning glare.

But Zak ignored our rage.

"Yeah, you know, I'm almost eighteen," he began, "and I heard about this sick commune up in the Dusk Mountains."

I smacked my forehead. A *commune?*

"I don't think you understand," Hael said. "We're going to help you discover who you *really are*."

Zak smiled. "That's why I'm going to the commune, man!"

"Who runs this commune?" I asked. Something about it smelled fishy to me...

"These two dudes who are real *rogues*, ya know? They're like 'fuck the system'! They got a real tight group of independents..."

I bit my lip.

Loch: Are you thinking what I'm thinking, brother?

Hael: Those motherfucking wannabes. Dane and Aneurin.

Loch: We'll make them wish they were never born.

Hael: You read my mind.

"Fine, then," I said to Zak. "Pack your bags by tonight."

"Wait, but—"

The little runt protested, but I had already moved on.

Hael and I left the garden and followed our favorite path into the forest. We walked briskly until we were under the cover of the trees.

And then we shifted.

I huffed smoke through my massive snout before launching into the air.

The sun was warm on my black, leathery scales. I felt the wind beneath my wings as we soared over the forest toward the Dusk Mountains.

As we reached mountain foothills, Hael and I began to circle, looking for this alleged commune. We didn't have to search long before we laid eyes on a black flame rising above the treetops...

Loch: The brothers are here.

Loch: And they have taken what's ours...

Hael: Showing mercy now would undoubtedly lead to problems down the road.

Loch: I agree.

Hael: Then there's only one thing to do.

Loch: We'll make them pay in blood.

Hael: Together, we'll teach them a lesson they won't soon forget.

CHAPTER 10: BROTHER DEAREST

MADDIE

I wandered through the dingy arcade, surrounded by flashing lights and the chaotic sounds of video games. When I had asked my estranged brother to meet with me, this wasn't exactly the location I was expecting.

But then again, if my recent behavior was any indication, I wasn't an expert at one-on-one talk.

My hang with Zayda had been a shitshow. When I woke up the next morning, I cursed myself for being so harsh with her and walking out. I mean, her boyfriend had just *died!* It was totally inexcusable.

But back on the rooftop with vodka in my system, I was fucking *pissed*.

I couldn't handle the way Zayda had shit-talked Freesia.

After all the visions I had had of the poor woman, I empathized with her. Even more—I identified with her.

Hell, it was even possible that I was her second coming!

Maybe I felt a little jealous that Zayda could have been too...

Whatever.

I needed to figure out more about my past, and that was all that mattered.

Which was why I was here, in the dusty arcade, peering down each dim row of gaming machines to find my brother.

Mason.

My brother had been nice to me during my short time at Xander University, practically a lifetime ago. But when I decided I wanted nothing to do with my father, I'd written him off too.

I hoped he wasn't pissed.

In the very last row of the arcade, I saw a towering figure playing the machine closest to the wall.

I couldn't make out his face, but he had red hair. Could *this* be my brother?

Mason would've had to have gained a lot of weight.

But he was the only soul in the place...

I continued down the aisle slowly.

The young man was fully absorbed in his game, so much so that he didn't notice me just a few feet away.

The neon lights of the game flickered on his face, and I saw for certain—it *was* Mason.

From the determination on his face, I knew I couldn't exactly interrupt him. I stood behind him, looking over his hulking shoulder.

In the game, Mason was a solitary knight fighting a fire-breathing dragon.

The graphics were old and crappy, and it was hard for me to understand how the game was prompting such dedication.

He pounded on the buttons and jammed the joystick madly, clearly at some crucial moment in the game.

The digitized dragon rushed forward, and the knight hit him with his sword.

The dragon's health bar lowered by one square.

The battle raged on with both the dragon and the knight taking losses to their health.

After a few minutes, I found myself getting swept up in the action.

I wanted the knight to win. To beat the dragon and protect the castle...

Finally, after a fatal blow, the screen zoomed in on the dying dragon.

Instead of rejoicing, as I had predicted, Mason let out a sound like a dying animal.

"Noooooo," he whined.

"You were the dragon?!" I asked.

He turned around and saw me.

"Of course," he replied. "That's how this game works."

His expression told me that he hadn't known I was behind him, but he also didn't care.

I gulped. Mason looked *a lot* different than the last time I had seen him. He'd gained at least forty pounds and had grown a patchy, unkempt beard. His body odor stung my nose whenever he moved.

"Um, how have you been?" I asked.

He didn't reply. He just gave me an expression that said, "Cut the shit."

He clearly wasn't ready or willing to tell me anything, although I was curious after seeing his transformation.

"Let's go talk," he said without enthusiasm.

He pushed past me, heading down the aisle to the back of the arcade.

There was a saggy blue corduroy couch in a corner. As we sat down, a wave of cigarette smoke came over us.

I couldn't contain myself anymore.

"Mason, this place is a *shithole!*"

He shrugged. "No one bothers me here."

Okay. My brother had been going through some shit. But neither of us were here for talk therapy.

"I asked to meet because I want to know more about my mother. *Our* mother," I corrected myself.

Mason sighed.

"What do you want to know?" he asked warily.

"Well, what was she like?"

My brother sighed again, as if that was a boring and difficult question.

"I don't remember her well," he began defensively. "I'm only three years older than you. Toward the end, she was really sick. She died in childbirth."

"She was sick while she was pregnant with me?"

The thought that I'd caused her sickness made me feel bad, even if there was nothing I could've done. I tried to dam up the sudden flood of emotions.

Mason nodded. "She was like...sick in the head. I remember she said some fucked-up stuff." He looked at his hands.

"What kind of fucked-up stuff?"

"Um...I don't know." He fidgeted. "I just remember it made me scared."

I stared at Mason. He had changed so much since he had been my evil father's protégé. I was glad he had gotten out from under Xander's thumb, but it was clear he was struggling.

Was it partly because of the disturbing memories of our mother?

I had so many questions, but he didn't seem to be the one to answer them. The memories were too painful for him.

There was only one person who could tell me what I needed to know. If I could get him to tell me the truth...

Xander.

"I should go, Maddie," Mason said. He looked exhausted as he pushed himself up from the couch.

I stood up with him and pulled him into a bear hug. "You take care of yourself, okay?"

"I will," he groaned.

He took off down another dark aisle of the arcade.

Alone, I found my way back to the light of day.

STORM

I soared toward the Dusk Mountains, the trees a green swirl beneath me.

I sensed some activity and needed to respond.

It was here that Silver had led Dane and Aneurin to build their lair.

From my outings around Requiem, I could see that the brothers were flourishing. If there was trouble, I wanted to know.

As I approached, I flew low to avoid detection. When I was even closer, I landed and shifted into my human form.

As I stepped over the stream, I heard the clash of tooth and nail...

A dragon fight.

I hurried on until I reached a clearing in the forest.

And then I could see them.

And I knew it was more than a rowdy scuffle...

It was a *Twin Leading Breed duel.*

Loch and Hael were vicious opponents as they maneuvered around Dane and Aneurin.

Their inherent connection allowed them to dance a deadly duet with their opponents.

Hael snapped at Dane's wing, making him flounder midair.

Aneurin plunged toward Loch with his talons extended, but Loch gracefully evaded the attack.

It was clear that Loch and Hael were playing the long game while Dane and Aneurin spent all their energy trying to engage them.

The mind-link buzzed with activity.

Loch: Recruit another young dragon, and we'll burn your pathetic commune to the ground.

Aneurin: The boy came to us!

Hael: Yeah, right.

Dane: You can't understand what t's like for someone to choose you of their own will.

Hael: Yet I always get what I want...

Loch: Get ready to eat dust, Dusk!

Already, the Dusk dragons were struggling with Loch and Hael.

I knew what the outcome would be.

Hael dove at Dane with his razor-sharp teeth extended. Dane twisted midair, but only enough that Hael's teeth met his side and not his belly.

With an air-rending rip, Hael tore through Dane's scales. The black dragon released a pained cry as he hurtled toward the ground.

With that, the duel was over. Aneurin soared down to care for his brother while Loch and Hael took to the skies.

I, too, retreated.

That the twins' rivalry should now come to a head intrigued me. The dragons of Requiem City were clashing.

The battle was over, and Loch and Hael had won.

But it only meant a greater war was imminent.

MADDIE

I lurked at the edges of the Xander University campus like a thief.

Why had I come here anyway?

My meeting with Mason earlier in the day had spooked me. I thought coming to the university might take me closer to Xander without actually having to be close to him.

But, in the dark, the campus held no clues.

I checked my phone. It was almost 11 p.m., and Loch and Hael would be expecting me at home.

I wasn't *avoiding* them, per se. I just wasn't rushing home. I hadn't seen them much since my little tantrum and wasn't sure how we would move forward.

As I rounded a corner, I saw the chapel that held Freesia's Rock.

It was surrounded by warning signs.

DANGER ZONE: BEWARE OF BLOOD

Just like in my vision!

Despite the warning, I ran toward the chapel and entered the dark space.

It wasn't only my vision.

Freesia's Rock was definitely, in real life, *bleeding*.

A pool of blood surrounded the stone. In this light, the liquid looked black.

Just like my vision.

Drawn to the grotesque sight, I crossed the grass from the shadows.

I stared down into the blood as it congealed in the open air.

It coursed down the black rock in a steady flow.

Before I knew what I was doing, I reached out and dipped my finger in a rivulet.

I rubbed the blood between my fingers, admiring its thick, velvety consistency.

I inspected it carefully, only to find it a deeper red than was familiar to me.

Was this human blood? Or...something else?

Suddenly, I heard footsteps outside. I hastily wiped my bloody finger on my jeans.

I needed to get out of XU. Now!

CHAPTER 11: SUMMER AT LAST

ANEURIN

I blinked my tears away. They were distorting my vision, and I needed to see clearly. Even if I didn't want to see this.

"It's going to be okay," I comforted my brother.

But I wasn't even sure if he could hear me.

Our battle was over, and Loch and Hael had taken to the skies.

Dane had shifted back to his human form. He was too weak to remain a dragon.

The gash on his side looked much more dire on human skin. Blood poured from the wound as my brother moaned quietly, trying to be strong.

Dane and I had welcomed many guests lately, and sometimes they stayed with us in our extra hammocks for many nights at a time.

But now we had no visitors. It was only us.

I had to find out how to help Dane, but I didn't know where to start...

Then it hit me. The pool!

I lifted my brother in my arms, groaning under his weight. I felt my skin become wet with his blood.

My legs carried us through the woods and over the stream.

Dane bobbed helplessly in my arms. The only thing that told me he was still alive was the soft moans I heard with each footfall.

"Stay with me, brother!" I whispered. We could speak with our minds, but words felt comforting right now.

At last, I saw the glowing green waters of the pond. I carried Dane the remaining distance and delicately lowered him into the healing pool.

My brother floated with his head above water. Still, his eyes were shut tight.

"Dane," I whispered nervously. "Do you feel any better?"

After a moment, my brother slowly opened his eyes. He looked as if he was traveling back to me from a faraway place.

I could see that he was still weak, but the pool had clearly revived him.

I reached out and turned him in the water. He rotated without complaint. His wound hadn't completely faded. The water had stopped the bleeding, but I could still see his red, exposed flesh.

"Let's wait," I told him. He responded by closing his eyes once more.

I sat on the bank beside my brother, praying that time would heal him.

After what felt like a small eternity, I turned Dane over. I winced when I saw red through the water. His wound was still open. The pool had helped him, but he wasn't healed.

"Dane?"

His eyes flickered open.

"I'm going to pull you out of the pool now, okay?"

He nodded. He was still too weak to talk.

I grabbed him under his arms and pulled him onto the bank next to me.

Kneeling, I propped up his torso on my leg.

I gazed down at his suffering face. I was out of ideas, and my brother still needed help.

I reached into my pocket. My fingers fumbled with the tiny keys of my cheap flip phone.

Even though I didn't want to get Maddie involved, and she never answered her phone anyway, she was the only person I could trust to help us. Even if her mates *had* put us in this situation to begin with.

I called her number and held the phone to my ear.

Please pick up. Please pick up.

The phone rang and rang.

"Aneurin?" Maddie said. She sounded like she was running.

"Hey!" I said. "Where are you?"

"Um...leaving Xander University. Really fucking fast."

"Oh, okay. I'm so glad you answered. I need your help."

"What's up?"

"Dane is hurt," I explained. "And we're in the woods."

"What?!" she said. She was still out of breath. "How did he get hurt?"

I paused. I didn't want to tell Maddie her psycho mates appeared out of nowhere to attack us, but that was the truth.

"Uh...Hael bit him."

"Are you *fucking* kidding me?!" she yelled.

I took that as a rhetorical question.

"I tried the healing pool."

"Fuck. Right. Okay, did it work?"

"It helped, but he still has a big gash. I think he'll probably need stitches."

I knew Maddie had stopped running.

"You have to take him to the hospital," she said. "But whatever you do, *don't* let them find out you guys are dragons."

I sighed, frustrated.

"Okay. But it's not like I can get an ambulance to come up here!"

I was freaking out. The healing pool had given me hope, but I had to face the truth. I couldn't heal Dane out here.

I had a big problem on my hands, and it was my responsibility to fix it.

"Um..." Maddie paused on the line. "How about you fly to a road? And then call an ambulance from there?"

"I'm worried Dane won't be able to hang on to me." It wasn't a bad idea, but if Dane fell off my back, we would be in even bigger trouble.

"Wrap him in your tail," Maddie suggested.

"Okay. Yes. Maddie, you're brilliant," I exhaled. I felt relieved to have a plan. "Thank you."

"Of course," she replied. "Call me from the hospital, okay?"

"I will," I said, hanging up.

I ran to grab some clothes for us both.

"Alright, brother," I told my semi-conscious companion as I pulled a T-shirt over his head, "we're going to get you help."

I stuffed my spare clothes into a backpack then shifted. I felt my body expand. My skin replaced itself with scaly armor.

I wrapped my brother in my tail, careful to avoid his wound.

When he was secure, I sprang from the ground. Together, we sailed over the forest. I landed on the first road I saw.

I shifted back and stood over my brother as I threw my clothes on.

We looked just like normal humans, right?

I could only hope.

I formed my alibi...

We were rock climbing in the woods, and then my brother fell.

Good enough.

I called the police and crouched beside Aneurin. Soon the flashing lights of the ambulance appeared, and the paramedics loaded us both on board.

SUMMER

My shift was almost over when the patient arrived.

At the end of a shift, nurses get worn out. Especially if they were ambitious—like me.

Though my inexplicable healing abilities gave me an edge, I still had to work hard.

I looked over the patient's initial report. He was a young adult male who had suffered a significant lesion on the right side of his abdomen.

I would inspect the patient, and if circumstances demanded, I would call in the surgeon. This was routine protocol.

I rounded the corner of the hospital, walking quickly to the emergency wing.

I pushed open the room noted on my clipboard, glancing one more time at the report.

"Mr... Dane?" I asked.

When I looked up, my heart stopped.

I was staring into the gold eyes of the most beautiful man I had ever seen.

His lips seemed to part in surprise as our eyes met. It was as if he recognized me from somewhere he couldn't place.

The man's physical presence was commanding, even as he huddled over his wounded twin brother. He gripped the other man's hand in his and held it close to his heart.

He was anxious, but for some reason, his presence made me calm.

I had treated handsome patients before, but never had I been so out of sorts.

"I, um...I'm Nurse Summer."

ANEURIN

I gulped.

The woman who stood before us made me mute and gave me a heart attack all at once. It was a good thing Dane and I were in the hospital.

The moment our eyes met, I forgot about my brother's circumstance. I forgot about everything. Even myself.

I existed only in relation to her.

Summer.

Her name was Summer.

"Aneurin," I replied. I held out the hand that wasn't holding Dane's.

She closed the space between us and took my hand. I felt warmed by her touch. And then calm.

"What happened to your brother?" she asked.

"A, um, rock climbing accident," I replied. "In the Dusk Mountains."

She inspected Dane's wound.

"Rock climbing in the dark?" she asked.

Fuck.

"Uh, yeah. It's a stupid hobby we have. We're competitive, you know. Twins and all."

She eyed me strangely.

"Okay..." she said. She returned her focus to the wound. "Something's not adding up for me here."

I couldn't help but smile.

"You think I would lie to a doctor?" I asked, giving her my best smoldering look. To my delight, she blushed.

"Well, I'm a nurse," she said, "but this wound looks as if it's about a week healed. Your brother's going to be okay. But a patient loses a lot of blood from a wound like this...I just don't understand."

Maddie told me to keep our secret at all costs, but I felt the urge to tell her the truth.

I felt I could trust her.

As I hesitated, she continued in a low voice, "If you tell me what really happened, I might be able to heal Dane without calling in a surgeon."

SUMMER

I eyed the dashing mystery man while I waited for his answer.

"Look, I can't tell you everything here," he replied.

The sentiment sent a shockwave through my body. The thought of meeting Aneurin outside of work thrilled me, but I pushed that thought away.

"But after Dane was injured, I took him to a healing pool. The water really helped him, but he was still hurt."

A healing pool?

"Where is this pool?" I asked.

"Dusk Mountains."

"Could you take me there sometime?"

His eyebrows raised, and then he nodded.

"Whenever you'd like," Aneurin said. His eyes were burning, and I felt my cheeks redden—not for the first time.

"Okay. Dane was really hurt before the pool, huh?" I continued.

Aneurin nodded again, gravely this time.

I sighed.

He told me a secret, so I figured it was safe to tell him mine.

"So, I'm a nurse. But I'm also a healer," I said. "I can help your brother."

Without waiting to see Aneurin's surprised expression, I placed my hands on Dane's side.

I closed my eyes, feeling the familiar heat course through my veins.

Energy rose from the ground beneath my feet, through my body, through my hands, and into the wound. I visualized skin growing over the flesh, the wound closing...

I drew one more deep breath, channeling the healing energy of the earth...

And then, when the procedure was complete, I opened my eyes.

ANEURIN

Dane's wound closed right before my naked eyes. His skin was good as new. As if nothing had happened.

I had recently been forced to accept that magic was real.

But watching Summer work, I had to rethink reality all over again.

Dane woke up, rolling over onto his back. He let out a yawn like he had just woken up from a peaceful catnap.

When he opened his eyes, he saw Summer. He instantly froze.

I knew what he was thinking.

He was wondering if he was dreaming.

He looked at me, and I raised my eyebrows.

Dane reached for his side to check his wound.

"You're all good to go, Dane," Summer said with a little smile.

When she got up to leave, it felt like I was losing a part of myself. From the look on his face, I knew Dane felt the same way.

Summer gave us one more backward glance before she left the room, taking my heart with her.

"Okay, brother," Dane demanded. "What the hell just happened?"

CHAPTER 12: DADDY DEAREST

MADDIE

Xander is a renowned academic and founder of Requiem City's most elite higher education institution, Xander University. I rolled my eyes and stuck out my tongue at the old photo of my father on his Wikipedia page. He wore lab goggles, and his bright red hair poofed into an Afro.

I scrolled past the lengthy descriptions of his scholarly works and accomplishments, the "important events" that took place at Xander University, blah blah blah.

The information I needed wasn't about Xander at all. It was about his wife.

Finally, I reached the "Personal Life" section. I scanned the paragraph until I saw it.

Serena Bowman.

Something seemed familiar about that name, but I couldn't quite place it.

Had I heard it in one of my visions?

The article said that she had died during the birth of the couple's second child, and that the child was lost as well.

Fooled ya, I thought to myself.

My mother's name didn't have a click link, so I typed it into Google.

The search showed articles about a family named Bowman and an archery competition, but there was nothing with my mom's name.

When I searched "images," I saw photos of a chimp named Serena who was apparently quite famous.

I sighed.

The search was proving unfruitful.

Had my mother lived her whole life under the radar?

Something told me that that wasn't true. I had a sneaking suspicion that Xander had erased everything about her.

Maybe so I couldn't find her...

Unfortunately, I would have to go right to the source.

I went to XU's webpage and found Xander's email address on his teaching profile.

I typed out a quick message.

Xander,

Need to talk ASAP. Write back.

Maddie

I was pushing back my chair when a response came in a few moments later.

Maddie,

Can you meet in my office in 30 mins?

Xander

I raised my eyebrows. The message had come so quickly...it was almost like Xander had expected that I would reach out to him.

At least it worked in my favor.

Yes.

I hit send.

Then I stood up from the desk in the library, grabbed my jacket, and walked out of the penthouse. My mates were at the orphanage, as usual. I still hadn't seen them since I had heard what Hael had done to

Aneurin...

Just the thought made my blood boil.

After Lochness was defeated, it felt like the three of us were on a honeymoon. That feeling had definitely faded. I always fell back into a state of distrust eventually. But maybe that's why I was such a good survivor, kind of like an indestructible, versatile city rat. Maybe it *was* what I *chose* to be. But fuck it, it worked, right?

Out in the city, the sky was gray and threatened rain.

I stomped the sidewalk in my combat boots. My thoughts were as stormy as the sky.

I thought of everyone I was frustrated with.

Xander was number one. After seeing Mason in such a dark place—mentally and physically—I knew there was one person to blame.

Our fucking father.

Xander had fucked me up by basically staying out of my life altogether.

I could only imagine what it must have been like to grow up under his care.

I was also mad at Loch and Hael for fighting with Dane and Aneurin. Why couldn't they just play nice? For once? For *me?*

I still hadn't heard the full story of how Dane had gotten hurt, but I was sure it was some stupid, macho, bullshit reason.

I rolled my eyes. *Twin Leading Breeds.*

The stupid drama.

I had had enough of that bullshit for a lifetime. The only thing that would make the situation more tolerable would be to have a girlfriend to laugh about it with...

Zayda crossed my mind. She came the closest to understanding me, but the last time we'd seen each other, I had stormed out of the room.

Maybe I had a little drama problem of my own...

Nah. Probably not.

The ground turned from concrete and asphalt to grass and groomed pathways.

The people around me turned from spiky-haired punks and coked-up businessmen to preppy rich kids.

I was approaching XU.

I shrugged, continuing on my way past the Xander University sign.

Make way for the second coming of your sacred bitch.

I bit my lip to hide my smile.

Then I saw the chapel.

My smile disappeared, and my jaw hung open.

The bleeding from the rock had gotten worse. So much worse.

The base of the building was red, as if the foundation had sponged up the blood.

Students crowded the chapel doorway to look inside, but I shoved my way through them.

The floor of the chapel was covered in a shallow layer of dark red ooze.

At the back, Freesia's Rock was covered in congealed blood. It looked like a big scab. A scab that couldn't stop its endless bleeding.

"Want me to push you in it, dragon bitch?"

Someone jammed their elbow in my back, and I nearly stumbled into the blood.

"Fuck off!" I cried, spinning around to face whatever evil twat had threatened me.

The blonde glared at me and huffed before turning away, pigtails bouncing.

"Goddamn no good piece of shit—" I began under my breath until I noticed a short guy standing beside me.

"Belinda's such a bitch." He shook his head.

"No kidding."

"She really did push someone in there," he said under his breath. "Apparently the poor girl had slept with her boyfriend."

"Shit," I replied. I didn't know who this guy was, or why he was risking his social standing to talk to me, but I liked him.

"She's still in intensive care now," he added with a big sigh.

"Wait, why?" I asked. Sure it was disgusting, but it was just blood.

He lowered his eyebrows at me. "You don't know? It *burns.* Like immediately. Third-degree burns."

He began to walk away. "I'm glad I told you, otherwise you might have gotten in trouble!"

What. The. Fuck.

I'd touched the blood already and was totally fine.

What did *that* mean?

I gulped.

Was this more evidence that I was the second coming of Freesia?

I rushed to Xander's office. I knocked on the door.

"Come in," he called.

I plopped down in a chair near his desk; only then did I look at my father.

He wasn't exactly *glaring* at me, but he wasn't happy to see me either.

"Madeline," he said.

For once in my life, I bit my tongue.

"Quite an exciting day on campus, don't you think?" he asked.

"It's a bloody mess," I quipped. "I'm surprised you're not cleaning it up."

He chuckled, though he didn't smile. "I suppose you don't know about the last time Freesia's Rock bled."

The last time Freesia's Rock bled...

My mind ran back to my vision earlier. Xander discussing the bleeding rock, here in this very office. But what did he mean? Had the rock bled before I was born?

"You might be curious to know," Xander continued, watching me carefully.

I didn't give him the satisfaction of asking.

I was here about my mom, not some stupid rock.

"I'm guessing you're here for information," Xander concluded.

"I want to know about my mother, Xander."

I glared at him, expecting him to shut me down. But he surprised me.

"I thought that would be it."

"Uh, okay. So will you tell me?" I asked.

"Oh, no," he chuckled again in his freaky way. "Or rather, only if you do something for me in return."

I seethed, gripping the arms of my chair.

As if this man didn't owe me enough already.

"What would that be?" I hissed.

"Bring me a piece of Dragonstone from Loch and Hael."

"I don't even know what that is," I replied, rolling my eyes.

"Then find out."

It was clear his patience was running thin. So was mine.

Guess I had something in common with this rat bastard after all.

"If I do this for you, you have to tell me everything I want to know about my mother."

He stuck out his hand.

"Deal. And I'll even tell you about the last time the rock bled."

Our hands only touched for a second, and even that made me squirm. I rushed out of his office immediately.

I leaned against the wall in the hallway. Seeing Xander always infuriated me, but all in all, our meeting could've been worse. At least he had agreed to tell me what I wanted to know.

As I exhaled, I felt like the life force was draining from my body.

I became very dizzy.

I staggered down the hall toward the bathroom. A vision was

coming on, and I didn't want to be all alone in the middle of XU when I went under.

I flung open the door and locked it behind me. I managed to lower my trembling body to the floor before the vision took over my consciousness...

It was dark.

The voices came muffled.

"No, I won't!" cried a woman.

"You will," came a far-off voice. "Make this easy for yourself, Serena."

The woman was my mother.

And the other voice was Xander.

In the darkness, I was terrified and alone.

"You can't force me to do that again!" the woman shrieked. "It's making me sick! And I'm carrying our child!"

Through the argument, I heard a loud heartbeat quicken.

Then I understood where I was. I was in the womb!

"Poor Serena," someone said from right beside me. The woman's voice was crisp and clear, not obstructed like the others.

I wanted to reply but couldn't. Who was next to me? I felt her presence, but it was too dark to see.

"I wish I didn't make her so sick," the woman said regretfully.

Then she began to sing...

"Loud is the blood

"As it lands in the mud

"When it spills from the black, cursed rock..."

I woke and slammed my hands onto the tile floor.

I crawled over to the toilet, where I expelled the sourness from my stomach.

I flushed my vomit away, struggling to catch my breath.

This was all so much worse than I had imagined.

In my vision, I was in my mother's womb. With *Freesia!*

Part of me didn't want to know anything more. But the other part was vicious with curiosity—the other part needed revenge.

But all of me needed to get off campus and away from my father *immediately.*

I opened the door and sprinted down the hall, out into the fresh air.

I kept running, passing the students gawking around the chapel.

I needed to get out of this hellhole. *Right fucking now.*

But then I saw something that stopped me in my tracks.

Through the open doors, I noticed a figure on the floor of the chapel.

Someone I recognized...

I moved toward her, forgetting everything I was running from.

I joined the others in the doorway, the horror on my face surely matching theirs.

Zayda lay on the floor, passed out in the pool of blood.

CHAPTER 13: BLOOD RED ROSES

ZAYDA

I felt so comfortable...as if I was sleeping on a bed of roses. I had a pillow of cloud beneath my head. And my lover was on the bed beside me.

Xythor.

My one and only.

He was alive again. I could just feel his presence beside me, which made me feel safe and sleepy.

And on my chest, I had our little bundle of love...

In my blissful and dreamlike state, I gazed down lovingly at the baby.

He batted gently at my breast with his little hand. He was almost like a tiny animal.

He began to cry.

I knew what this meant. My baby was hungry.

I noticed my swollen breasts. What a wonder that so many women have fed their children like this since the beginning of time. They didn't even complain from being sucked dry.

I, too, now bore the supreme duty and responsibility of raising a life.

The mothers' duty was also mine.

Dreamily, I lifted my baby up to nurse.

He clawed at me with his tiny fingernails and latched onto my nipple with his sucking mouth.

Sharp pain pulled me from my philosophical thoughts.

Was this pain normal? My baby clawing and biting me like some animal?

I looked down to see my baby staring up at me. His eyes were red and burned with a strange fire...

I screamed out of fear. Had I given birth to a monster?

Xythor tried to comfort me.

"Zayda!" he said.

"Zayda!"

"Zayda!"

I wrenched open my eyes.

"Zayda!" Maddie screamed.

"Oh!" I cried. I realized I wasn't sleeping in a bed of roses.

I was lying in a pool of blood.

And I had just had my most fucked-up vision so far.

Not that it was much worse than the real world. After all, I was covered in blood.

It slicked my hands, soaked my shirt, and drenched me through to my underwear.

Maddie had it on her, too. Red splattered her face, probably from the effort it had taken to wake me up.

I struggled to my feet on the slippery, blood-soaked floor.

"Let's get out of here," Maddie cried.

And then we took off running.

My body ran on animal instinct. The blood terrified me. The sheer quantity of it was repulsive. The way the puddle grew so quickly and unpredictably felt almost...evil.

The rock was like the grave of a huge, dead animal.

The blood squelched beneath my sneakers as we ran out of the chapel.

A huge crowd had gathered, whispering among themselves. Nobody tried to help us or see if the blood had injured us.

No. They were glaring. Gossiping. Plotting.

As Maddie and I ran off campus, the image of the students' cruel faces burned in my mind. I knew what they were thinking.

They hated us. They wanted us to burn.

They were angry and frightened that we'd escaped from the blood unscathed.

The students of XU were used to magic. But when they looked at us, they saw something different. Something dark. Perhaps even evil.

And maybe they were right.

"Let's go to mine," I said, leading Maddie down the sidewalk.

Though Maddie and I hadn't exactly left things on good terms, none of that mattered now.

"Thank you for waking me up." I met her eyes and gave her a little smile. Maddie sighed and shook her head, letting out a small laugh.

We were okay now. Even if Maddie and I were oil and water, fate kept making sure we stayed friends.

People stared at us on the street. I crossed my arms over my chest, as if that could help to hide the fact that I was drenched in blood.

"Should we just run there?" Maddie asked.

"Definitely," I replied with a laugh.

"Last one there's a rotten egg!" shouted Maddie, taking off like a rocket. We raced all the way to my apartment. When we arrived, there was no way to keep blood off the floor.

No one else was home, so we stripped and threw our clothes directly in the trash. There was no saving them.

We didn't even need to ask whether we would shower together. We both just needed to get clean as soon as possible.

Maddie and I piled into my shower, and I slid closed the glass door.

I twisted the faucet, and the water came.

It was cold at first, but it felt blissfully good. I pulled Maddie toward me, toward the stream. I watched blood rinse off our arms.

It felt like a baptism.

But the ceremony was tainted by the confusion of what had happened. The anxiety of what our futures held.

And, as we smiled at each other under the falling water, our gaze was charged with love and gratitude.

We were both thankful not to be alone.

MADDIE

I plopped down on Zayda's couch and sank into it like sand.

Finally, after the shower water had stopped running red, and we'd cleaned up all the blood and taken the bag of clothes to the trash, the whole thing was over.

Zayda handed me a mug of tea and sat down at the other end of the couch. I pulled up my knees so that my feet were on the cushion, and my back leaned against the arm.

"What a day," I sighed.

Zayda held her mug and breathed in the steam.

"You know people get burned by the blood, right?" she asked.

Okay. She wants to get right into it.

I nodded.

"I just don't understand it," she went on. "One minute I was standing, and the next I was—having that vision..."

"What were you doing at XU?" I asked bluntly. I knew I shouldn't have been short with Zayda, but I'd just pulled her out of a pool of blood.

"What were *you* doing there?" she shot back.

"I was there to find out about my mother," I answered through gritted teeth.

"Well, did you?"

"No. I have to do something for Xander first."

Zayda waited for me to elaborate. I didn't.

"What do you have to do?" she touched her forehead, frustrated. "You know what, Maddie? This is only going to work if we're totally open with each other. We have a lot of shit to figure out, and maybe together we can actually do it."

I considered this and then sighed. "Fine. But you go first."

Zayda nodded and looked into her mug.

"Well, you know how I have visions of the future?"

I nodded.

"I think my visions have become more intense since the rock started bleeding. I want to know if you feel that way too."

She paused as if she were organizing her thoughts.

It was an interesting idea. And it rang true for me too.

"Earlier today," Zayda continued. She leaned toward me, like that would help us to connect. "I had a vision that I was nursing a baby..."

She dropped her head, starting to cry.

"That's sweet, Z," I said, trying to comfort her.

She looked up at me with bloodshot eyes.

"It's not really sweet. I'm pregnant, Maddie."

I felt the blood drain from my face.

"With Xythor's—?"

Zayda nodded.

"Oh my God! Will you keep it?" I asked.

"Of course I'm fucking keeping it," Zayda responded. "It's the last piece I have of Xythor."

"Right. I'm sorry." I shook my head. Why did I have to be so insensitive?

"It's okay. It's just...stressful, you know? Because in my vision, this baby wasn't totally human..."

I held my breath as my mind raced. The only other Blood Mage I knew who had borne a dragon's baby was Freesia...

And we all knew what had happened to that one.

"It will be okay, Z," I comforted her, reaching to touch her knee. Of course, I didn't know for sure.

"Well, I have hope. Which leads me to the other thing I have to tell you."

Zayda swallowed. She looked like she was about to be sick.

"I'm bringing Xythor back," she said.

"What?!"

What the hell did that mean?

"I'm bringing him back from the dead. Xander said he would help me, so—"

"Oh, so *this* is why you're working with Xander!"

I shook my head. Zayda was in mourning. She wasn't thinking straight. But how could she be so fucking *stupid?*

"And what do you have to do for him in return?" I asked. I knew my voice was sharp as a blade, but I didn't care. I wanted to cut.

"He takes my blood," Zayda whispered. "It's so he can revive Xythor's body."

That was enough. I couldn't believe that Zayda had agreed to give her *blood* to that disgusting degenerate. He was lower than a worm.

I stood up, accidentally knocking over my tea in the process.

"Are you a fucking idiot, Zayda? You think this is going to work?!"

"In my visions—"

"Fuck your visions!" I shouted. "No wonder you're passing out all the time. Who knows what that two-faced bastard is *really* doing with your blood? You could be putting other people in danger, Zayda. But you're too selfish to think of anyone but yourself."

Zayda was quiet. Once again, I knew I was near the point of no return.

"Maybe you're forgetting, Maddie," Zayda hissed, "but you're working with Xander *too.*"

"Oh, fuck off!" I shrieked.

That was different. *So* different. And for Zayda to attack me when she was gambling with her life...

"Zayda, I can't do this. I can't handle your *fucking* drama; I don't want anything to do with it anymore."

My friend's face crumpled before my eyes, but I didn't care.

"Maybe you're the next Freesia, or maybe I am," I said in a low voice, "but we're each going to have to figure it out alone."

Zayda started to cry, but I didn't wait around. I stormed out of her apartment and out into the evening.

Alone in the street, I knew I'd said my piece. But it didn't make me feel any better at all.

CHAPTER 14: A WELCOME DISTRACTION

MADDIE

When I got back to the penthouse, I strode right toward my dressing room. I was still wearing Zayda's clothes, which felt sort of fucked-up and wrong.

It had been a hellishly long day, and my solitude comforted me like a fuzzy blanket.

Once I had on my comfiest sweats and my oldest tee, I curled up into a ball on the couch.

All I wanted was to fall asleep, but my mind was racing.

Zayda was pregnant.

Even though I had gotten so pissed at her, I couldn't imagine how difficult carrying her dead boyfriend's child must be.

I wondered if her baby meant that she was the true coming of Freesia...

The rock wasn't just bleeding anymore. It was *gushing,* and soon it would flood the whole campus. Maybe even the entire city.

Something big was coming. That was the only thing I knew for sure.

But if it was a war, who would be its soldiers? And why had Xander insisted that I learn about the last time the rock had bled?

I sighed. I still needed to figure out what the hell Dragonstone was.

I sat up, my eyes wide open. There was no way I would be able to sleep right now.

As nice as it was to be alone, I was starting to get sick of it.

I knew just what could distract me: Letting two dragons ravage my body. Now, I just had to find out what my mates were up to...

In my arousal, I almost forgot that I was mad at my mates for hurting Dane.

My friends had texted me that Dane was okay. In fact, their trip to the hospital was a blessing in disguise. Apparently they met a new friend there—a woman.

But that didn't mean I would let Hael and Loch get away with it.

I padded down the marble hallway looking for them.

"Loch! Hael!" I called.

"Here, mouse," came a voice from the library. I followed it. When I entered the room, I saw my mates bent over that stupid board game.

I groaned. If the past were any indication, it would take a tornado to pull Loch and Hael's attention from their new favorite pastime.

"Hey guys," I called.

I ran my finger across Hael's massive shoulders. Then I stood behind Loch and began to massage his back.

"Give us an hour, mouse," Loch said. Neither of them even looked up from the board.

I wonder if these fuckers realised not paying me any attention made me even more needy.

"Nope," I said. "I want answers now. Why did you guys attack Dane and Aneurin?"

They both glanced up at me.

"We had to assert our dominance," Loch replied, cocking a brow, as if that was normal.

"Well, I'm pretty fucking mad about it. Dane had to go to the hospital!"

"We weren't trying to kill them, rat. Just warn them." Hael shrugged. "Stop fretting. He's okay, right?"

"Yes..." I said, my arms crossed. "Promise me you'll never hurt them again."

Hael scoffed.

"I mean it!" I yelled.

They were silent as they returned their attention to the game.

"Fine, mouse," Loch drawled, clearly amused by my distress. "Now they're scared of us, so we won't need to."

Okay? Huh. That was easier than I had expected.

"Cool..." I replied awkwardly. "So...can we hang out now?"

"In an hour," Hael repeated.

"Ugh!" I cried out as I plopped down on the couch nearby. My head was spinning from my talk with Zayda. "Um...I actually need to talk."

It was as if the spell had been broken. Suddenly, I had the full attention of my mates. They both turn to me immediately.

"What is it, mouse?" Hael asked, concerned.

"Tell us," Loch murmured seriously. Perhaps they thought I'd gotten into another street fight. For once that wasn't the case.

"You know how I told you I might be the second coming of Freesia?" I asked.

They both nodded, listening intently.

"Well, apparently it might be Zayda instead."

My mates frowned. I gathered my strength and went on.

"But...I want it to be me. I'm worried that she can't do it. And I want to be the one to break the curse and save the dragons of Requiem...to save *you*."

It was the first time I'd said it out loud, and I immediately felt better. Loch and Hael stood and walked over to me.

"Of course it's you, street rat... your destiny is a curious thing," Loch whispered, pulling me into his arms.

"Not to mention, there's no way Zayda is more powerful than our big, strong mouse," Hael smiled handsomely as he kissed my cheek. "We're right here, and we'll help you the whole way. Don't you worry, Madeline."

My troubled heart felt whole again.

Loch's and Hael's beautiful, haunting eyes fixed on me like I was the only thing in the world. My lips parted as I let out a shaky breath of sudden desire.

I pulled my mates close and stayed there for a moment between their strong chests.

Sure, lately I'd been lusting for a normal relationship...but there was no way normal could feel as good as *this.*

They were strong, possessive, and even willing to help me conquer the world if that's what I wanted. I loved them so much my heart hurt. I found it hard to express how warm and protected I felt right then.

"Thanks, guys," I whispered, blushing. "Now finish your game so we can hang out."

They each kissed me and returned to their seats, resuming the game where they had left off.

I watched them as they stared at the board. Immediately, they became stock-still, clearly in a deep mind-link conversation.

But it was almost like they were listening...to the game.

Finally, after nearly two minutes passed, Hael moved one piece forward one space.

"So, what do you guys call this game again?" I asked.

"Dragon's chess," they replied at the same time, though neither of them looked up at me.

"What's it like...made of?"

"The pieces are pure gold," Hael said.

"And the board is made of onyx and Dragonstone," Loch added.

My ears perked up at that last part. I craned my head to get a closer look...

The board was checkered with black stone that was definitely onyx. The other was glowing and milky white. The Dragonstone, I assumed.

Hmmm.

I knew I couldn't exactly take the board to Xander. The brothers hardly took their eyes off of it.

But at least now I knew what to look for...

I gazed at my mates, who were consumed in their precious game. Both of them rested their elbows on their knees, and their biceps bulged deliciously.

I'd agreed to let them finish, but their sweetness had turned me on, and my patience was starting to wear thin.

How hard could it be to distract two dragons?

Leaning back on the couch, I lifted my leg in the air. My loose sweatpants fell slowly, and I fingered the hem as it gathered around my knee...

Loch glanced in my direction.

"Your turn," Hael insisted. Loch looked back at the game.

Ugh.

They were deep in it. I would have to pull out the big guns...

I skipped out of the library and back to my dressing room. Entering my walk-in closet, I knew I would need an extra special outfit.

I pulled open a velvet-lined drawer and lifted out the leather collar that was studded with sapphires and diamonds.

I hadn't worn it before; now seemed as good a time as any. I fastened the heavy snap at the back of my neck and looked in the mirror.

Oh, shit.

I looked sexy as fuck with my wild red hair shining against the sapphires.

Inspired, I pulled open my underwear drawers. When I'd moved in, Loch and Hael had supplied my closet with the sexiest lingerie money could buy.

It wasn't exactly my *thing,* plus I hadn't wanted to give them the satisfaction, so I had ignored it.

But now, I was in the mood. I spent a good five minutes squeezing my ass into a pair of black latex panties. They had a zipper from the back to the front...

Then I fastened on the matching bra, which was so tight that my boobs all but spilled out of it.

The outfit was restrictive, and I felt my skin begin to sweat under the unbreathable material, but I found I liked the sensation. It made me *hot.*

Finally, I strapped on a pair of platform stilettos.

Let's see if you'd rather play your game now, boys...

I strutted down the hallway once more, making sure my heels clacked loud enough for my mates to hear.

When I arrived at the library, I stretched my arms across the doorway and struck a pose...

The brothers' heads swiveled toward me.

And then their mouths fell open.

Oh, yeah...

They stood up immediately and prowled toward me. But I wasn't their prey. I was their match.

"Shall we take a little break from our game, brother?" Loch asked, his voice dry with lust, on the edge of a full growl.

"I think we could manage," Hael replied carefully, his eyes glued to the collar around my throat.

The brothers grabbed the fronts of their t-shirts and ripped them off of their chests at once, like co-stars in some steamy Chippendale show. On their bare torsos, they wore two matching leather harnesses with big silver rings in the center.

My mouth fell open.

Apparently, I wasn't the only one who had dressed to impress. We were clearly on the same frequency.

My mates looked hot as *fuck,* and even more dominant than usual.

I devoured them with my eyes. Hael let out a growl as he watched me.

I practically pranced forward and grabbed their harnesses, pulling them into the hall. Their bodies pressed against me, and I could feel their erections through their matching leather pants.

"I demand a meeting in the treasure room with the Dobrzyckas," I purred before turning on my heel and continuing my catwalk.

I could practically feel Loch's and Hael's eyes burning holes in my latex panties.

I spun the lock on the door, and then we all dove into the treasure room.

Immediately, the brothers pounced on me. They kissed and bit my neck, running their hands over my skin and skintight latex.

In the frenzy, I pulled on the clothes I could reach, trying to lift the tattered remains of their shirts off of my mates...

Loch kissed my neck deeply, nibbling on that one spot that got me every time.

While they were kissing me, I peered over their heads. And in the display cabinet against the wall, I noticed a collection of milky white rocks...

Dragonstone.

I smiled, losing myself in my mates' affection.

When I opened my eyes again, their pants were gone. As always, their perfect bodies made me breathless.

Their swollen cocks were ready to fuck me *hard*. Hopefully at the same time.

"Perfect," I growled while biting my lip.

Loch and Hael moved toward me, pushing me until the back of my knees felt smooth leather.

But instead of falling back, I hung from their harnesses like monkey bars, letting them support all of my weight.

"Down, mouse," Loch whispered, and I finally dropped onto the antique couch.

Reclining, I stared up at my hungry lovers. Their massive erections pointed down to me.

Hael began to stroke his length as I squirmed under their gaze, feeling the delicious leather on my skin.

"Take off my shoes," I ordered.

"No way, mouse," Loch said.

"You're leaving *all* of that on," Hael added.

I shrugged. Oh, well.

My mates joined me on the couch, one on either side. They pulled my breasts from their latex cage, and I reached down to massage their shafts.

"No, mouse," Loch drawled a command, "let us guide you."

I relaxed my body, giving myself to the feeling of their hands squeezing my ass and trailing lightly down my stomach...

With one satisfying *zip* the center of my underwear fell away.

The cool air on my most sensitive skin electrified me. When the initial shock wore off, Hael stroked my opening before plunging a finger inside me.

Oooooh.

I arched my back as Loch climbed over me and positioned himself between my legs.

"Yes," I cried as he tapped his rock-hard cock against my clitoris before settling it at my slit. With one swift movement, he thrust inside of me.

A delighted scream escaped my throat. How long had it been since I'd had my mates?

Why did this feel so *fucking* good?

Loch bucked inside me, holding my hips and pushing his fingers under the skin-tight fabric at my hips.

Hael was on his knees next to my head, and I licked my lips as I stared up at his massive cock. He was stroking it gently with his hand, and I saw a drop of wetness on its perfect tip.

I pushed myself up on my elbows and took his tip in my mouth.

He moaned but continued working his shaft with his own hand. With his other, he pinched and caressed my nipple.

I closed my eyes, feeling Loch move skillfully inside me, working shallowly but quickly up into my G-spot.

With Hael in my mouth and my breasts in his hand, my brain overdosed on pleasure and horny thoughts.

"I'm going to—" I cried.

"Cum," both brothers encouraged, as my orgasm rippled through me like a nuclear bomb of ecstasy.

I moaned with my lips still on Hael's cock.

He continued to stroke himself. From the way his ab muscles were tensed, he was close to his climax.

"Fuck me however you want," I moaned up at Loch.

He began to thrust at a frantic rhythm, his eyes roaming hungrily between my breasts and my pussy...

Seeing these sexy men so turned on brought me close once more, and Loch's repetitive motion stimulated me in a whole new way.

I was going to cum again.

And my mates knew it.

"*You're finally behaving*, you gorgeous brat," Loch *had* to tease me, even managing a smirk.

I tipped my head back, giving myself over to my imminent orgasm.

Hael moaned and released all over my breasts, and I felt Loch's seed burst inside of me.

And then, along with my mates, I felt pleasure rock my body for a blissful second time.

STORM

I prowled the perimeter of Xander University in my beggar disguise.

From the shadows, I glowered at the evil place.

If I could burn it down, I would.

But that was not why I was here.

I had been waiting for the blood from Freesia's Rock to trickle outside the campus grounds. Finally, it had.

The chapel that held the rock was flooded, and a moat of blood surrounded the building.

War was coming faster than I'd anticipated.

But some things were still uncertain.

I knelt to the ground and pulled an empty vial from my pocket. Careful that the cursed blood wouldn't touch my skin, I scooped up some of the oozing liquid.

I tucked the sample away and disappeared back to the shadows.

It was time to see just how dark our future would become.

CHAPTER 15: DANGEROUS GAMES

ZAYDA

I woke early to the birds outside my window and groaned.

Somehow, even the sun made me feel worse.

The world was full of happy people, but I wasn't one of them.

It was no surprise that I woke up sad, because I'd gone to sleep crying.

After Maddie had left, I'd sat on the couch until the tea went cold in my hands.

I was waiting for Thea to come home. Or Harry. Hell, even Darshan.

I tried to look casual in case someone poked their head in.

"What's up, Z?" they would ask, throwing themselves onto the couch opposite me.

"Oh, you know... Just facing never-ending tragedies..."

I didn't make it that far in the fantasy.

Really, I wasn't in the mood to be fun. I would've broken down in tears if someone had asked me to hang out. But at least I wouldn't have been alone.

Around midnight, I finally went to my bedroom.

I knew I shouldn't have let Maddie affect me so much.

But despite all the signs that suggested otherwise, I'd held on to the hope that when I told her everything, she'd understand.

She'd say, *I would have done the same thing.*

And in turn, I would have listened to her problems and comforted her.

But it hadn't worked out like that.

In the face of Maddie's rejection, I'd reckoned with my decisions all over again.

Of course I knew some were unwise, but I wouldn't take them back even if I could. I needed Xythor.

I knew he would have done the same if I was the one who had died...

MADDIE

I woke up late, nestled in between Hael and Loch.

I rolled onto my tummy and put one hand on each of my mates' chests.

"What's for breakfast?" I asked. "Pancakes? Bacon?"

Loch's eyes drifted open.

"What time is it, mouse?" I checked the clock on the side table. "Ten."

"We have to leave," Hael said with his eyes closed.

"Why?" I pouted.

I'd had so much fun with my dragon lords the night before that I wanted to keep the party going.

And hanging out with them was my favorite distraction. I didn't have to think about the rest of my problems.

"We're teaching a class in an hour," Loch explained.

Teaching a class. Yeah, right.

"You mean playing that stupid board game with the orphans?" I asked.

Hael smiled, rubbing his eyes.

"Sounds like someone doesn't like when they're not the center of attention..."

"No!" I shouted defensively.

They shared a glance.

"Actually, we're teaching the kids how to care for the garden, so we don't have to hire a gardener."

"Fine," I said nonchalantly, hopping out of bed. "Hope you lizards have a good day."

"Not so fast, mouse..." Loch managed to grab my hand. "Come here."

He pulled me toward him until his face was only an inch away.

Even in the morning he didn't have bad breath. How was that possible?!

"Kiss me," he ordered.

I meant to stay angry and just give him a peck, but he kissed me so sweetly, his lips moving softly over mine, his tongue tracing the outline of my mouth.

Despite my best, most stubborn intentions, I gave myself to our kiss, remembering how sexy he'd looked in his leather harness—and how hot the sex was afterward.

When I finally pulled back, I was startled to feel Hael's chiseled back behind me.

"How—?" I asked.

But then I was lost in another equally intense and tender kiss.

When the second one was over, Hael smacked my ass.

Loch leapt up and got dressed, and Hael threw on an effortlessly sexy and sophisticated outfit. Before I could catch my breath or get a word in, my mates were out the door.

"Humph," I said to myself when they left, crossing my arms over my chest.

How was I going to keep myself busy without them?

I flopped back onto the bed and stared at the ceiling.

My thoughts whirled madly. I wondered what Zayda was up to at that very moment...and Mason...and even Xander.

What did my evil father do in the morning? Eat nails for breakfast and slaughter a kitten?

That's it!

I knew exactly what I would do with my day.

No, not slaughter a kitten...

I would find the Dragonstone for my evil father.

I sprang from bed and put on some clothes. I took a handful of bobby pins from the drawer of my vanity.

Then I made a fancy espresso in the kitchen. I still wanted pancakes, but I didn't want to make them alone.

I settled for a bowl of sugary cereal. Then I continued on my way to the treasure room.

I'd memorized the code my mates used for the keypad by the metal door. I typed it in quickly and stepped into the immaculately clean space.

The chrome details of the sex equipment glittered in the low light, and the black leather couch reminded me of what we had done there the night before...

I forced my attention back to my project. The display case.

Behind the glass, I saw a shelf filled with Dragonstones.

These were the only items in the whole cabinet.

I gulped. My mates would definitely notice it was missing...

I resolved to just take the smallest one. When I tried to pull open the door, however, it didn't even budge.

Of course the thing was locked, but there was a way to open the case, right?

With my fingertips, I searched the outside for a lock. When I couldn't find one on either side, I stooped to the floor.

The cabinet stood on four legs, so it was slightly elevated.

I reached my hand underneath and felt a metal opening.

Yes!

I positioned myself under the cabinet and peered up into the opening.

"Huh?" I said aloud.

I had picked a fair number of locks as a youngster but had never seen anything like *this.*

The keyhole was large and round. The cavity was smooth and curving.

I didn't even know where to begin.

I reached into the hole with my bobby-pin, but it only scratched along the metal walls of the keyhole. I needed to find another strategy if I wanted to get inside.

Hmmm...

I pushed myself out from under the cabinet and sat on the floor.

The hole looked like it was meant for a small object.

The key wouldn't look like any old key, so it could be hiding in plain sight.

I thought of jewelry and little knickknacks, but I was pretty sure my mates didn't have any of those things.

"Oh my God!" I shrieked.

I burst from the treasure room and into the library. There was that stupid game. Dragon's chess. But today, it might just help me out.

I leaned over the table, inspecting the pieces.

Each one was unique, but their shapes were curved and round.

Was one of them the key?

I took a few pieces in my hand and returned to my position beneath the cabinet.

I tried one, but the top was too large to fit in. Then I tried another, and another. Finally, I picked up the last piece I'd brought.

Just when I was about to get more pieces to try, I gently rotated the piece in my hand.

The glass door clicked open above me.

"Yessss!" I cried.

I lifted the heavy glass door and reached inside. I grabbed the smallest stone there was. It was smaller than the palm of my hand.

I gazed at its milky-white surface. It looked like liquid was shifting inside...

Just by holding it, I could sense its magic.

What in the hell was Xander planning to do with it?

STORM

I took the vial of blood to the deepest part of the forest. Around me on either side were miles of woods.

Here lay the stone that I needed.

It was the largest Dragonstone within the borders of Requiem City. A surface about the size of my forearm showed through the soil, but like an iceberg, much more of the stone stretched deep beneath the ground.

I was focused as I set about my test. It had been more than eighteen years since I had last performed it.

I arranged the ingredients around me.

I placed the freshly harvested rabbit's foot at the top of the arrangement.

I laid the ferns down delicately. When the traditional pattern was complete, I poured the blood into the center.

The dark red liquid hissed and bubbled when it hit the rock, boiling on contact.

I shifted to my dragon form and lowered my humongous snout to the shrine I had created.

By blowing a controlled blast of dragon's fire over the blood, I completed the final step.

The flames instantly burned the whole display away, and black smoke began to billow from the blood.

The scent was disgusting and stung even my dragon eyes.

Smoke filled the forest. It billowed over the treetops into the sky.

I hadn't expected this outcome. It told me that the dragons' task would be extremely difficult.

Our opponents were formidable. Our victory was not promised, as I had assumed.

The spirits, wronged so long ago, were demanding change.

War was on the horizon. It was as near as the rising sun.

The reckoning was coming fast, and it was coming for us all.

CHAPTER 16: HIDING IN THE DARK

MADDIE

"Tell me what you feel," Darshan said. I'd managed to slip out of the penthouse without Loch or Hael noticing that anything was amiss.

But I didn't necessarily expect to come back to my old apartment and witness this.

Darshan was on the couch next to Thea, who was wearing a blindfold. He held a stuffed elephant that she was feeling with her fingers.

"I feel something round," Thea said as she touched the ears. "And soft. Really soft."

"Okay, good so far," Darshan replied.

I needed to get rid of the Dragonstone that was literally burning a hole in my pocket with its pulsating magic.

But this scene was just too much to pass up. I didn't know when I'd get another chance to watch Thea feel up a stuffed doll.

I found a half-empty bottle of cheap chardonnay in the fridge and poured myself a full glass. I settled into a chair across from the two lovebirds.

"Don't mind me," I said. "Just here for the show."

"God, this is embarrassing," Thea said.

"Focus on what's in front of you," Darshan said. "Pretend it's just you and me."

Thea went back to feeling the stuffed elephant from trunk to tail. Finally, a glimmer of understanding sprouted on her face.

"It's Mr. Bubbles!" she shouted. "My little elephant!"

She held the stuffed doll to her chest and hugged it tightly.

Ugh. I wasn't drunk enough for this.

I took a large gulp of the wine and felt its gentle fizzle settling into the pit of my stomach. I was about ready to leave when Darshan pulled out the next object.

"Okay," he said, smiling, "the last one."

My jaw dropped.

If I hadn't seen it with my own two eyes, I wouldn't have believed it. The object Darshan held was...

A pink dildo!

I laughed into my hand to muffle the sound. Thea's blindfolded face turned in my direction.

"What's so funny?" she asked.

"Nothing," I said. "Just can't wait for Mr. Bubbles to meet his new friend."

"You're gonna ruin it, Mads!" Darshan said.

Thea turned back to the task at hand and reached out with her fingers. Her face knotted into a mask of confusion.

"It's an odd texture," she said. "Feels like rubber. Maybe silicone. Did you bring home one of your cooking utensils from work?"

Oh, fuck. This is deliciously painful to watch. And I love it.

"Sure, it's made from the same material," Darshan replied. "Maybe feel the whole length of it."

Thea complied. As her fingers moved to the tip of the dildo, her eyebrows arched in understanding.

"Oh, fuck no," she said. "Please tell me you didn't."

But he *did!*

Thea ripped the blindfold off her eyes. Her cheeks flushed beet red with embarrassment.

"Darshan!" she screamed. "You told me you found random objects from my room. This is not random!"

"I grabbed whatever I could find. You're the one who left it lying around," he replied.

I couldn't hold it back any longer. I rocked in my chair, laughing hard and loud.

Darshan joined in my laughter. Thea lightly smacked him on the arms and legs, but to my surprise, she wore a big smile too.

Soon they were holding each other, their lips locked in a passionate kiss.

It had been hard at first, getting used to my friends being together. Now I could see what made them such a good couple. They were having fun while trying their best to understand one another on a deeper level.

Shit. What was that kind of a relationship like?

It was difficult to imagine my two lovers taking an interest in my passions or hobbies. But I couldn't pretend they weren't trying. I never thought I'd see the day when they changed their mansion into an orphanage.

I finished the glass of chardonnay and left it sitting on the living room coffee table. Thea and Darshan's kisses had become wet and sloppy. I was glad they enjoyed one another so much, but their open PDA was starting to make me nauseous.

I entered my old bedroom and closed the door behind me, making sure it was locked. For extra security, I closed the blinds and checked that the mint bracelet was tight on my wrist.

Since I'd been spending so much time at Req Tower, Thea and

Darshan had converted my room into storage. Random boxes and knick-knacks littered the room.

It made me feel slightly homesick, thinking that my friends were already beginning to move on without me here.

I opened my closet and dug through the old clothes piled on the floor. After a few moments, my fingers found my old backpack.

I dumped out the contents inside, which included school supplies, an empty water bottle, and a half-eaten energy bar.

This bag would only need to serve one purpose...to safely transport the precious stone.

I only had designer bags back at the penthouse. I needed to hide it someplace normal. Inconspicuous. Maybe my old bag would make me look more like a student, so I could avoid some of that homegrown Xander University tension.

My hand wrapped around the Dragonstone in my pocket. I immediately registered the magic in its touch.

Its milky-white hue filled the dark room with a cold glow. For a few moments, I sat staring at the stone, mesmerized by its beauty.

I wrapped it in a thin cloth and set it into the backpack before zipping the bag closed.

Xander would get what he wanted. But would I finally get to learn about my past and, more importantly, my mother?

I hoped Xander would keep his end of the bargain...

LOCH

Something felt different.

After we arrived back at the penthouse, it took nearly an hour to fully register the disturbance. But the feeling was unmistakable... it was as if Hael and I were missing pieces of our souls.

"What could it be, brother?" Hael asked.

I closed my eyes and tried to pinpoint the disruption, but it was no use.

"I don't know," I admitted. "But we're going to have to search for whatever's been misplaced."

"Our little mouse is still wearing her bracelet, and her speciality is thieving," Hael continued. "Perhaps if we can convince her to remove it, we'll have clearer heads."

I chuckled at his insinuation. Maddie had been acting much differently lately. But as much as I wanted to, I couldn't quite pin all the blame on her.

My descent into Lochness had tipped the scales of our relationship. Even though we'd recently rekindled the spark, it still wasn't a full flame.

If Maddie was the reason for our sudden unease, it was cause for concern. Sometimes she seemed as if she'd never entirely give herself to us.

"Let's solve this nagging problem," Hael suggested. "Or I might start to go crazy."

Hael took the lower floor of the penthouse, searching like a crazed bloodhound for whatever could be throwing us off balance.

I checked the floor above, starting with our bedroom. As always, it was immaculate. It only took me a few moments of searching to realize it was a waste of time.

The sensation was certainly greater on this floor, but I couldn't yet put my finger on why.

I decided to wander the hallway and passed a few rooms that gave me no indications. I began to follow the steps up to the treasure room when an intense feeling of emptiness seized my heart.

I pressed our code into the keypad at the metal door. When it slid open, I stepped inside, letting the piles of gold and jewels overwhelm my senses. I never tired of the rush I experienced entering this room and laying eyes on all we had claimed.

I walked through the room, touching the silk fabrics and counting the pictures to make sure nothing was amiss. Suddenly, a glint of light from the cabinet caught my attention.

As I approached the case, a terrible knot formed in my gut.

Inside, our collection of Dragonstones glowed with unmatched beauty. Even the piles of gold lost their luster when compared to the magical stones.

But not all of it was there. One small stone was missing.

Dragonstone was an ancient gem that had the potential to harness great energy and power. Dragons like Hael and I could gain strength from it. But in the wrong hands, the stones' magic could be used against us.

If someone like *Xander* got his hands on the stone, it could be dangerous for all dragons...

Loch: Brother!

Hael: What is it? Did you find anything?

Loch: Come to the reasure room at once!

A wisp of smoke filled the room, and Hael's figure formed at my side.

"Please tell me you found an intruder," he said. "I'm starving and wouldn't mind a human-sized snack."

I shook my head and pointed at the display case.

"It seems as though the intruder already left," I said. "With quite a haul."

Hael studied the Dragonstone cabinet until he spotted the same discrepancy I'd discovered.

"We're missing a piece of the stone," he muttered. "Fuck..."

He looked at me again with fire in his eyes.

"Was it Maddie?" he asked angrily. "Did that little rat really bite the hands that feed

her?"

I shook my head in disbelief.

"She wouldn't," I said. "Not after everything we've given her."

But who was I kidding? Maddie had defied us more times than I could count. *Just when I thought the brat was learning to behave.* It would be just like her to try to get the upper hand in a situation.

Unless...

"She has been keeping company with some unsavory characters," he said in disgust.

"The twins," I replied.

Hael nodded his head.

"Those fucking drug addicts," Hael snarled. "They're going to pay for stepping foot in this penthouse."

I cracked my knuckles and felt my jaw clench tight.

We'd beaten Dane and Aneurin in battle, and it seemed as though they were already begging for another ass whooping. Of course they'd put Maddie up to something like this. They wanted some of our power and were too cowardly to face us themselves. I bet they asked our sweet mouse for a favor and she obliged to be kind. She had a soft spot for mongrels.

Those dragon wannabes would pay for this.

Hael and I would keep spilling blood until they fucking learned to stop messing around in our territory.

CHAPTER 17: VISIONS OF THE CURSE

ZAYDA

I stared at the countless vials, all in various colors. It was as if a leprechaun had showed up in the middle of the night and dumped the colors of the rainbow into each sample.

Only it wasn't a child. These vials were collected by a mad scientist who wished to see every dragon wiped from this world.

Every test tube held a concoction with a different purpose. Some were for healing, while others were for sedation. Or worse, I imagined.

A select few were colored in hues of black and brown.

Were these potions made for killing?

I touched a few of the vials and felt their strange warmth. It was as if the liquids inside were actually alive.

I sat down in a chair at my station and rested my forehead on the desk. It had been a long day.

Hell, who was I kidding? Since Xythor's death, each passing day felt like it had dragged on into eternity.

And after my latest fight with Maddie, it seemed as though we'd never repair our friendship. It felt like the weight of the universe was sitting squarely on my shoulders.

Moments like these were when I would've gone home to Xythor's waiting arms. He always knew how to comfort me, no matter the problem. His warm smile and dazzling eyes were all I needed to see.

I wiped the tears forming in the corner of my eyes and cleared my throat.

That was all in the past now. No matter my perception, time moved quickly, and I had to learn to move with it.

I turned on the small desk fan and let its breeze blow over my face. Earlier I'd given more blood to Xander. He'd promised me it would be all he'd need for a while. It was a relief to hear.

Giving so much blood had taken an unbelievable toll on my body. If there was anything I needed more than Xythor, it was a fucking vacation.

Somewhere tropical. With cold water, soft sand, and enough alcohol to keep me on cloud nine for a week...

I closed my eyes and tried to imagine being on a remote island. I could almost feel the tropical breeze blow across the beach, rustling palm tree fronds.

Frothing waves crashed on the shore. Each time a new wave rolled in, a different sound echoed in my ears...

A baby's crying rode the fresh evening air. The sound was piercing and unpleasant, but this was my baby. I needed to soothe his pain.

It was a beautiful little boy, with a crop of curly, black hair. He was beautiful; he looked just like me.

I tried to rock the child back and forth, but it did no good. His mouth never seemed to close shut. It was an ever-gaping hole bellowing horrific wails that refused to stop.

With a free hand, I exposed my breast and lifted the baby's mouth to my nipple. My little boy turned away, unsatisfied with my attempts to appease him.

"Please, there must be something to make you relax," I whispered to him.

His eyes looked into mine, and once again filled with tears that cascaded down his chubby cheeks.

I had to do something.

A melody began to sound in my head, distant and unrecognizable. As I continued to rock the baby, I tried to hum the broken tune.

At first, it was a disaster. My voice was uneven and cracked as it regurgitated the song. But as I continued to warble through the notes, everything fell into place.

"Oh, Dark is the wind

"When it blows through the cave

"And the wolf gets the poor shepherd's flock.

"Loud is the blood

"As it lands in the mud

"When it spills from the red, cursed rock..."

I'd never heard those lyrics in my life. But they came to me as if I'd written them myself.

It was bizarre—and yet wonderfully familiar all the same. Every breath I took brought a new set of words that sailed the short distance between my baby and me.

Part of me wanted to stop.

But I couldn't stop. It felt so...right.

As I continued to sing, the little boy in my arms quieted down and stared at me intently, as if he understood the gravity of my words.

His eyelids began to flutter until they could no longer stay open.

By the end of my song, I was astonished to be looking at a sleeping baby. Not only that, but I somehow felt rejuvenated from the effort.

The words had given me a jolt of life. I had the sudden desire to stand up and fly into the sky.

"Thank you!" I whispered to the clouds above. "Thank you for hearing my prayers."

❖

I woke up to my desk fan blowing directly into my face.

What in the hell did that mean?

I stood up from my desk and stretched my aching muscles. It was hard to wrap my head around what had just taken place. Of course, it was just a dream.

But to have a dream of that magnitude...it was as if I had actually been holding a child in my arms. That was more than any reverie or fantasy I'd ever had before.

It must have been some kind of premonition.

And that song.

My body shivered just from the thought of it. It made me feel so... *powerful*. The words were so frighteningly clear in my mind. But why?

The ghostly melody still pulsed in my ears, haunting my waking thoughts.

"When it spills from the red, cursed rock..." I sang quietly.

Hearing the words out loud gave them an even more powerful meaning. And what the hell was a cursed rock?

My eyes widened as I realized the answer...and it could be found on this very campus. *Freesia's Curse!*

Once again, my world was turned upside down.

Not only had I dreamt about giving birth to a dragon baby, now I'd been given the words to Freesia's powerful song.

No wonder Maddie had reacted so harshly to hearing about my visions. If there were ever signs about the second coming of Freesia, these would definitely qualify.

I shook my head, hoping these new realizations wouldn't cause my brain to explode.

Maybe working overtime has started to take its toll. That beach vacation couldn't come soon enough.

I decided it was best to gather my things and head home. If I stayed any longer, I might end up making a mistake I couldn't fix.

My footsteps echoed off the tile floors. No one else was in the lab at such a late hour.

The sensors caught my movement and turned on one light after another. It was an eerie feeling of being watched when no one was actually there.

I pulled my backpack tighter around my arms and tried to pick up my pace.

Then I heard something...

It was the song from my dream. But it wasn't playing in my head. It seemed to be coming from a room down an adjacent corridor.

My brain told me to head to the elevator and get the hell out of this spooky lab, but my gut told me to check out the source of that wistful song.

I took a deep breath and, against my better judgment, headed down the adjacent hall.

The rooms I passed were dark, and I could see my reflection in the windows—tired and a bit unsettled.

Just needed to confirm that I'm not hearing things. Then it's off to bed, and I won't wake up until I'm good and rested.

I stopped at a room at the end of the hall. There was nowhere else to go. As I reached toward the handle, the music had all but stopped.

This is stupid. Turn around and go!

I grabbed the knob, and to my surprise, it was actually unlocked.

So much for security clearance...

The door opened with a hiss. I listened for the song but could no longer hear any trace.

I stepped inside the darkened room and was expecting to see a closet filled with janitorial supplies.

Sensors caught my presence, and the light flickered on.

It was a relatively empty room, save for a table that looked to be littered with papers.

As I drew closer, I saw that the papers appeared to be blueprints.

Maybe they contained a new wing for the laboratory, or perhaps a health center for students to work out?

Who was I kidding? Xander was too fucked-up to plan something so useful for his students.

I picked up the nearest set of papers.

What the fuck?

It was several sketches of dragons. And from the look of it—these were no ordinary dragons...

They were robots!

I wanted to believe that some student had left some crazy art project behind while killing time between classes. But the heading at the top of the paper told me otherwise.

Xander Laboratories: Prototype for a Robotic Dragon.

The measurements of these robots looked to be huge... At least fifteen feet tall with a wingspan doubling it...

I looked at the other blueprints and found more of the same. They were all slightly different but had similar intentions.

Holy shitballs!

Was Xander planning some type of robot dragon army?!

CHAPTER 18: GIVING UP THE STONE

MADDIE

Here we go again. I stepped onto the campus of Xander University. It had seemed like ages since I'd last visited of my own free will. But in reality, it was only a couple of days.

The university grounds were as beautiful as ever. The lawns were green and manicured, while the ivy on the buildings glistened with a fresh coat of morning dew.

But the beauty was just a facade. Within these buildings were some of the most dedicated young dragon slayers anyone could hope to teach.

I continued walking and tried to swallow my apprehension. But the crimson I saw soaking the grass nearby wasn't helping to calm my nerves.

What in the...

I stood on the sidewalk for a moment in complete awe. It looked like a massacre had taken place, but most students were going about their day as usual.

The only variation was to give the bloody swamp a wide berth.

My gaze found the old chapel at the epicenter of this weirdness. Apparently, Freesia's Rock was still spewing blood; it had gotten much worse since my last visit.

Suddenly, a dark and ominous energy overtook me.

Every student I passed stopped to stare. They knew my face and what I stood for. Hell, a picture of me was probably posted on a dartboard at the student union.

My stupid backpack wasn't helping *one bit!*

I'd run from these little hellions while they tried to skewer me with knives and smash me with books. Obviously I'd prevailed, but that didn't make me any less angry.

If that curse was ever broken, I'd want revenge as much as Loch and Hael would.

I made my way to a towering building made of gray stone. Once inside, I took the stairs up to the fourth floor and stopped in front of two massive mahogany doors.

Xander's office.

I half expected to see Nautica blocking the entrance. Xander's right-hand bitch annoyed me almost as much as his boss. After all, the little shit had nearly shot me...

It took me a moment to realize that the entire floor seemed to be empty.

I knocked on the large doors.

"Come in," Xander's voice called.

As I entered, I was met with a blast of icy air. It felt good after trudging through the heat outside.

But the significance wasn't lost on me. The room was as cold and unwelcoming as the person who inhabited it.

Xander was standing at his window, staring out at the campus. The sun's rays outlined his figure in gold.

I almost laughed at how angelic the demon looked.

"Welcome, Madeline," my father said without turning around. "Please, have a seat."

"It's Maddie," I corrected. "And I'm just fine standing."

Xander turned around and looked at me through his wire spectacles.

"Ah, yes. I forget how independent you are," he said with a half-grin.

"I've never forgotten how cold and calculating you can be," I replied.

The grin was instantly wiped from his face. He cleared his throat and moved to his desk, taking a seat in an oversized chair.

"Let's get down to business," he said. "I assume there's only one reason you came back."

I nodded my head and unzipped the backpack, reaching inside a hidden compartment. I felt the magical pulse of the Dragonstone on my skin.

For a moment, I didn't want to hand it over.

There was something about its odd warmth that bid me to keep it close...to never let scum like Xander anywhere near it.

My father's gaze was hard and laser-focused.

I shifted in place.

Being in the old bastard's company had passed the uncomfortable part. Now it was downright excruciating.

He held out his hand, annoyed at my hesitance. My fingers left the stone in the backpack.

I would give it to him, but he had to give me what I wanted first.

I plopped down in the seat across from him and flashed my sweetest smile.

"Before you get this beautiful stone," I said, "I want some answers."

Xander leaned back in his chair and touched the tips of his fingers together. I could practically see the cogs turning in his fucked-up mind.

"Do you even have the stone?" he asked sharply.

I felt the gem once again in my fingers and lifted it into view.

The expression on his face instantly changed.

The gem's milky white hue lit the lenses of his glasses, giving him a crazed appearance.

I let the Dragonstone mesmerize the old man for a few extra seconds before stuffing it back into my bag.

His face returned to normal.

It's not like he couldn't just snap his fingers and have a slew of dragon slayers descend on me. But that move wasn't in his best interest.

I'd already agreed to steal the stone from my mates and bring it here to Xander University. There was no way off this campus unless Xander allowed it.

"Where should I start?" he asked.

I gathered my courage and leaned forward.

"At the beginning," I said.

Xander nodded his head as he spread out his palms on the desk.

"It's been a very long time since I've talked with *anyone* about her," he admitted.

"Well, there's no time like the present."

"Indeed," he replied. "And I suppose I owe you as much."

Owe me as much...

He gave me up to an orphanage and then tried to murder me... he owed me a whole hell of a lot more than that!

"In the beginning, it was perfect," he began. "I had everything one could ever want: a wonderful son, the love of my adoring wife, and a budding university filled with bright students."

My hands balled into fists. If everything was so perfect...then what the hell happened?

"But when your mother became pregnant with you, things began to change," he said.

I couldn't ignore the sadness in his voice. It wasn't often that a megalomaniac like Xander actually opened up about his feelings.

But there was an edge to his words that didn't go unnoticed either.

"Of course, blame it all on the orphan," I said, annoyed.

"It was her dream to raise a little girl," he said. "And I was overjoyed to see your mother so happy. But then the visions began to plague me."

Visions?

It seemed like everyone was plagued by dreams and premonitions in this city. Must be something in the water...

"What visions did you have?" I asked.

"Ones concerning Freesia," he answered.

My breath was choked from my lungs. First it was Freesia's Song, and now my father was having visions of her!

These *had* to be signs that I was her second coming!

"I dreamed of the cursed rock, oozing blood. I dreamed of dragons descending from the sky. And most of all, I dreamed of Freesia creating the curse with her baby's blood."

I shivered in my seat. It wasn't from the cold air, but from Xander's steely voice.

"You have to understand how these visions plagued me," he said. "Stealing my sleep and haunting my every waking hour."

"We've all been haunted by nightmares," I said. "How were these any different?"

Xander smiled cruelly.

"Because they weren't simply nightmares," he answered. "I believed they were premonitions of the second coming of Freesia."

I gasped at his words. Xander noticed my reaction.

"I tried too hard to force her second coming into existence. One night, when the visions were worse than usual, I visited the rock and extracted a sample of the blood...Freesia's blood..."

My body was frozen with anticipation. I *needed* to hear what had happened to my mother.

"With a needle and syringe, I injected Freesia's blood into Serena's womb," he said.

I gasped. I knew my father was a crazy fuck, but this took it to completely new levels.

If he could do such a thing to his own wife...he was capable of *anything.*

But then my thoughts shifted to the syringe filled with blood...

I was the baby in her womb.

"That would mean that..." I stammered, unable to finish my sentence.

"You have Freesia's blood running through your veins," he answered. "In fact, Freesia's Rock last bled on the day that you were born."

I was in complete shock. Had Storm been right about me the entire time?

With everything Xander was saying, it seemed like I was the real second coming.

"But it was a mistake," Xander said coldly. "The blood made your mother sick. Over time, it drove her unbelievably mad. By the time Serena was in labor, it was too late."

Xander's head dropped down as he looked back on his dark memories.

"Your mother died giving birth to you. A *cursed child.*"

Cursed child?

"But you're the reason for my curse!" I yelled.

"Yes, which is why I gave you to the orphanage. I hoped to get you out of our lives for good."

Ours...meaning he and Mason...

I felt another flush of anger race through my body.

"But when you resurfaced, it frightened me. You were a failed experiment. I thought it was only right to end what I created," he said.

"Father of the fucking year," I snapped.

He nodded his head in sad agreement.

"It was an act of uncertainty. But I realize now that you are stronger than I could have ever imagined," he replied. "Your mother would be proud of you."

I stood up from the chair so quickly that it toppled over. I pulled out the stone and slammed it on his desk. A deal was a deal, even with the devil himself.

As Xander's attention was distracted by the golden glow, I made my exit.

He didn't even try to stop me.

I rushed down the stairs and out into the humid heat of the day.

What did it all really mean?

If I was just a failed experiment, how could I be the actual second coming of Freesia?

Could it really be...

Zayda?!

CHAPTER 19: FUN AND GAMES

LOCH

I tried my best to hold back annoyance. The little orphan we had picked out was working on the board game. But it wasn't looking good.

There were times it appeared he might choose the right piece. Other moments it seemed as though he might surprise us and make a bold, unexpected move...

Each and every time just led to failure.

All dragons loved children. That was a fact that none of us could deny, even Twin Leading Breeds. But when a child consistently failed to meet our expectations...

I clenched my jaw tight and ground my teeth.

Ever since we'd lost Zak to Dane and Aneurin's horde, it'd been impossible to find a suitable recruit to replace him.

This little towheaded squirt just wasn't getting it.

Hael shook his head in disappointment as the child again chose the wrong piece.

Loch: This is no use, brother.

Hael: You don't have to tell me twice.

Loch: Our chances of building a victorious horde are getting slimmer with each passing day.

Hael: So much for these damn orphans.

Loch: What should we do now?

Hael: What else can we do? Stay put and hope this imbecile actually starts to get it.

I looked at the boy once more. He alternated glances between Hael and me. It was as if he were trying to read our thoughts.

Fat fucking chance that will ever happen...

MADDIE

The taxi pulled into the circle drive of the mansion. I stepped out into the fresh air and stretched my limbs.

It didn't matter how often I visited this place. It was always breathtaking.

What made it seem even more special was the fact that my mates had turned it into an orphanage full of Requiem City's lost youth.

But now they were finding their way.

As I looked at their hopeful faces, I found a peace that had evaded me for quite some time. It was comforting being back with kids who shared my broken background.

My memories flashed back to my early years with Darshan and Harry. We hadn't expected to make many friends in the orphanage. That made our relationship even stronger when we realized how much we had in common.

It would have been amazing growing up in a mansion like this outside of the suffocating bustle of Requiem City.

Then again, none of these children knew the Dobrzyckas very well.

I watched as a young girl tried to juggle a soccer ball in the air. She looked so happy to be playing in this beautiful place that she could call home.

My heart should've been warmed with affection for my two mates. They had allowed all of this to happen. And without even consulting me!

But I couldn't shake the feeling that something was wrong. My mates had never showed this much attention to anything besides sex, money, and power.

They might be *teaching* these children, but I worried what it was these children were starting to learn.

I followed a path that led around to the back of the mansion. Immaculate hedges and beautiful flowers filled the garden.

I kept following the footpath down past the gigantic playground and through a grove of trees. It was such a beautiful day. My ears were filled with chirping birds and the gentle splash of a water fountain.

This was like a beautiful dream. I wanted to stay in it forever.

The path eventually broke into a fork. I stood trying to decide which way to go: toward a lush labyrinth, or a secluded rock wall.

I wasn't in the mood to get lost, so I walked toward the wall. Children's laughter echoed off the rock.

There must've been some sort of fun happening. I didn't want to disturb the kids, so I tiptoed over, hoping to watch them play without interrupting.

Several children were lined up, their faces lit with smiles. A woman sat on a patch of grass as she guided the children through the game.

But who the hell was she?

"That's right, little ones!" her familiar voice called out.

"Just follow me."

Adara!

Last time I'd seen her, she had been teaching the children gymnastics.

But what did today's lesson include?

I continued to watch as Adara spread her arms as wide as possible. The children mirrored her movements.

Adara then roared into the air, her quiet voice suddenly booming. Some of the children flinched, but the majority watched in awe.

It was like they were doing exercises or some type of calisthenics. But why was she roaring?

"Don't be afraid," she told them. "Dragons are never afraid!

Oh, fuck no. She's trying to teach them how to act like dragons!

Adara gave another roar, this time much quieter than before.

The children who had initially been scared started to grow confident. They tried out their own little roars.

At first, it was absolutely adorable seeing the youngsters flex their muscles and growl like dragons.

Then, one of the young girls started to steal the show.

Her body began to tremble, and her jaw opened wide. I watched with alarm as it unhinged, and her teeth grew into small fangs that dripped with drool.

Her cute little growl had turned into a full-on roar.

I gasped, and Adara finally spotted me...

"Well," she said, "it looks like we've got ourselves a spy."

I stepped forward. The kids stopped and stared at me with apprehension.

"And what would I be spying on?" I asked pointedly.

Adara turned to the children.

"Great job, everyone. You're dismissed. We'll pick up again this evening," she said.

The children burst into cheers and sprinted past me. I watched as they bounded up the path toward the mansion.

"They're coming along quite nicely, aren't they?" Adara asked.

"Well, I can't argue that they all look happy."

"It has been said that happiness is the best medicine."

I scoffed. "I'm glad you can run this orphanage on laughter."

Adara shook her head in annoyance.

"This orphanage is run by the wealthiest family in all of Requiem City," she said. "The students will get the best of everything. Isn't that what you wanted for them?"

Adara pushed past me and headed toward the mansion. Her long strides made her move quickly, so I had to hustle to keep up.

"What was that back there, then?" I asked. "I saw that girl..."

I couldn't quite find the right word for it...

"Nearly transform," Adara finished.

I nodded my head, starting to understand what was happening.

"It's not the first time I've seen something odd happening with the children," I said. "Last time I was here, Loch and Hael were playing dragon's chess with them."

"Then you saw their best versions," she replied.

"What the hell is that supposed to mean?"

"Dragons love children," she said. "Something's mesmerizing about their innocence. It draws us in and soothes our souls."

"I find that hard to believe," I replied.

Adara stopped and stared at me.

"My brothers have the best intentions for the children at this orphanage," she said, annoyed. "But that also includes discovering the special ones."

The special ones?

"You mean like that girl," I said.

Adara nodded.

"Dragon's chess helps determine who has the potential to be a dragon," she admitted. "It's been used by dragons for centuries."

I could feel my head swimming as I tried to comprehend all the new information I was receiving.

"Why the hell do they want to discover more dragons?" I asked.

It didn't make sense. Loch and Hael greatly injured Dane when they first met. The fact that they were dragons only made their dislike that much stronger.

"Are they trying to weed out more dragons to...to exterminate them?" I asked nervously.

"No, of course not. They're trying to find more so they can start a horde," she replied.

A horde of dragons...that sounded like the last thing this orphanage needed, much less Requiem City.

Adara smiled as she watched me try and decipher the meaning.

"I thought you were smarter than this," she said.

"This is a lot of fucking information," I admitted.

"Poor little lab rat, your brain can't take it all."

My instinct was to punch her, but I knew that wouldn't help me in the least.

"Tell me what's going on!" I demanded.

"Requiem City has held us down long enough," Adara said. "With a horde of dragons, we can finally take it back from Xander and his dragon slayers."

I should have seen it from the start. Of course, Loch and Hael couldn't defeat Xander and his minions on their own. They needed help!

Just like them to need something and not admit it...

However, Adara's answers made one thing even more uncertain.

Why did Xander need the Dragonstone?

Did he know that the Dobrzyckas were coming for him?

I hoped I was wrong.

By giving Xander the Dragonstone, had I just tipped the scales in his favor?

CHAPTER 20: BUILDING THE HORDE

MADDIE

The next few moments seemed like a blur. I followed Adara up the steps but could no longer think of anything else except the Dragonstone.

If these children really were dragons, I'd just given a monster the means to end their lives.

Adara asked if I wanted to join the children for lunch, but I couldn't answer. There was no way I could be around any of those kids in my current state.

I stumbled around the perimeter of the mansion until I could see the circle drive.

My hands fumbled for my phone. I was finally able to pull up a ride-share app and searched for a nearby car to take me back to the city.

"Leaving so soon?" Loch's voice called out. "Don't you want to stay for dinner? Hael and I have a special dessert we'd love to share with you."

Loch and Hael were standing at the top of the steps leading to the mansion. I walked farther out into the circle drive, feeling the gravel crunch beneath my feet.

"I don't want to talk to either of you," I said.

"What a moody little mouse," Hael replied. "But you're more than comfortable speaking with our sister."

I turned and faced them. They both had self-satisfied smiles on their lips.

This was precisely what they'd hoped—to draw my attention away from what I really wanted to do. *Leave.*

But damned if their little distraction wasn't working.

"Adara had some interesting things to tell me," I responded. "Don't you find it odd that your sister tells me more about you than either of you do?"

Loch and Hael descended the steps.

"Do you have something you'd like to tell us?" Loch asked.

"You've been just as secretive as we have lately," Hael added. "Do we need to take you to the treasure room and pry it out of you?"

I could feel my brand burn with desire. Yes, *of course* I wanted them to pry it out of me. But I was still mad enough to see through their sexiness.

"Forget it," I said. "I'm not staying here any longer."

"What's wrong, mouse? Don't you want to see how the orphanage is doing?" Loch asked. "You love it here."

"Oh, I think I've seen enough for today," I replied.

"When you're wearing that mint bracelet, we can't read your mind," Hael pointed out. "Why don't you just tell us what's bothering you? If you want to communicate so badly, don't forget it's give and take, little rat. Give something to us in return."

I didn't want to give them the satisfaction of telling them everything. But if I kept my thoughts inside, they would eat away at me until they made me sick.

"Fine! I'll tell you exactly what's bothering me," I said.

The twins looked at one another with the slightest of smiles.

"For one, I'm pissed that it never seems like I get a choice in my own life," I began, annoyed. "Find a nice man with mutual interests?

Nope! I have a lifelong bond connecting me to two Dragon Lords."

Hael opened his mouth to counter. I gave him a look from hell, and his mouth promptly closed.

"For another, I can't believe you would actually stoop so low as to use the guise of helping kids to find fucking *dragons!*"

They shared another look before moving closer.

"You misunderstand our intentions," Loch began. "We're not doing anything to harm these children."

"On the contrary," added Hael, "we only want what's best for them."

I laughed at the deranged idea that these two manipulators could possibly know what was best for any child, let alone a whole orphanage full of them.

"We're trying to find and educate the orphans that might be dragons," Loch continued. "But it's for a greater cause. Something is happening in Requiem. We need to form a horde."

"Of course you do!" I retorted. "It's all about what the two of you need. Who cares about a bunch of kids with no parents?"

"Please, Maddie," Hael said.

"Why couldn't you just tell me the truth?" I said. "I love both of you. Yes, I get fucking pissed off. And yes, you make me want to rip my hair out! But you don't have to lie to me or keep your lives a secret."

"That goes both ways!" Loch snarled. "You willingly wore the collar, rat. You know what this relationship entails."

"You've been pulling away from us more every day." Hael replied. "What's wrong, little mouse? Is there something you want to tell us?"

I gulped. Okay, sure. I'd stolen the Dragonstone. I didn't like sneaking around behind my mates' backs, but we didn't exactly have a *normal* and *healthy* relationship most of the time.

Being the third wheel to two Twin Leading Breeds wasn't easy. But maybe I could open up more if they weren't so damn arrogant all the time.

"Come back to the penthouse with us," Loch suggested mischievously. "We'll make it all up to you."

"That's a promise," Hael replied. "We'll even let you pretend to be in control for a while."

"A hard spanking might get you back on track, too," Loch added. "Then we'll decide how many orgasms to give you. Come on, little mad love, *relax for once*."

They both chuckled.

My brand burned more intensely than before. Going back to their penthouse wasn't the *worst* idea. And I hadn't been alone with them in so long...

However, I shook my head.

It was just another trick to win me over, and this time it wouldn't fucking work.

"No! This is it!" I yelled. "You won't talk me out of this. I don't agree with what you're doing here. You can't just fuck me over to your side every time. I'm leaving, and I'm not coming back! Bye!"

Hael started to say something, but I wasn't listening. My ride pulled into the driveway, and the gravel that crunched under the tires drowned out Loch and Hael's complaints as they bitched to each other about me. Fuck them and their moods.

I got into the car and slammed the door shut.

I needed to get away from my mates.

I needed to find Dane and Aneurin.

ZAYDA

"I'll have a mimosa," Thea said. "And make it strong."

"Make that two mimosas," Darshan replied.

The waitress nodded her head and looked at me.

I smiled, hoping that I wasn't about to make things too awkward.

I'd agreed to meet Thea and Darshan for a Saturday brunch

hangout. What I didn't anticipate was for them to be tipsy before I'd even arrived.

I wanted to see two of my best friends, but for me, alcohol was *not* on the agenda.

"I'll just have some sparkling water," I said.

As the waitress walked away, I saw the looks on Darshan's and Thea's faces.

"Boo!" Thea said, already tipsy. "Don't be a buzzkill."

"I'm not!" I replied, already annoyed.

Thea's face dropped as she realized her mistake.

That's right, dummy. I'm pregnant. You were there, remember?

"Alright," Darshan added. "Then don't be a brunch kill."

I shook my head and tried to think of something to throw Darshan off the trail. He was a good friend, but I didn't want *everyone* knowing about my pregnancy.

At least, not yet...

"I had some bad fish last night, and my stomach is still recovering," I lied.

Ugh. And what a terrible lie it was.

From Darshan's groans, my fib seemed to be working.

"Well, just avoid the Baja tacos, and you should be good," Darshan said.

"Ohmygod—but their Baja tacos are sooo good!" Thea replied.

The waitress came back to the table with our drinks, breaking up the awkwardness of the moment.

I took a sip of my water and reveled in the tiny bubbles of carbonation exploding in my mouth. This topic needed to change—and fast!

"I can't believe the date of your wedding is arriving so quickly!" I said.

"I know!" Thea squealed. "It's all happening so fast."

"But that's a good thing, right?" Darshan asked.

"Of course it's good," I replied. "It's wonderful. I just can't help but think of how much our lives have changed in just one year."

"There have been a lot of changes," Darshan agreed. "But it's not all bad. Look at us! Still making time to hang out. That's everything you could ask for!"

I smiled at Darshan's positive attitude. Maybe he was right. Things have been changing, but that didn't mean it was negative. Nothing stayed the same forever.

I took another sip of my water, and this time, the feeling wasn't so pleasant. My stomach did a somersault followed by a cartwheel.

"Excuse me," I said quickly.

Before they could react, I was out of my chair and headed toward the ladies' room.

I barely closed the stall door before a torrent of fluid erupted from my mouth.

Fuck! Not again!

Morning sickness. And it was the second time in as many hours.

I flushed my vomit down the toilet and washed out my mouth in the sink.

My face looked several shades lighter, but there was nothing else I could do. I splashed cold water on my cheeks and forehead before heading back out to meet my friends.

"Was it the Baja tacos again?" Thea asked, winking.

Good thing Darshan was blind, because she was terrible at keeping a secret.

"Yeah, you look like hell," Darshan added. "I'm assuming..."

I wanted to smile at his stupid joke, but I was too weak to try.

"Girl," Thea added, "Tell me you're doing okay."

I looked into her eyes and was amazed at how focused she was, even after finishing another strong mimosa.

Thea was one of my best friends. No matter how tipsy she got, it never seemed to weaken her friendship radar.

"I'm fine," I lied.

She nodded her head, but I could tell from the look on her face that she *knew* something was up.

I wanted to tell her everything: about my plan to resurrect Xythor, my big fight with Maddie, and the visions that constantly haunted me.

But the drunken brunch celebrating their engagement just wasn't the time.

I shook my head and took a few gulps of water.

"I'm fine," I lied again. "Really, believe me."

XANDER

I listened to the whirr and grind that filled the small laboratory room. Upon receiving the Dragonstone, I'd ordered a gemstone cutting machine. It had arrived earlier in the day.

For the last hour, I'd watched in delight as the blade sliced the small white stone into tiny shards. It was beautiful beyond words.

Finally, I had something of the dragons that I could use against them. And it would forever tip the scales in my favor.

My fingers grasped one of the shards, no bigger than a piece of candy. I felt its edges prick my skin and grinned with delight.

I walked to a sanding machine and flipped the switch. After a few more minutes of work, the stone was as smooth as a piece of silk.

Under the harsh halogen lights, the polished gemstone glowed brighter than ever before.

Of course, leave it to me to improve on something from a fucking dragon. How ironic that a gemstone delivered by Loch and Hael's mate would be the eventual downfall of their kind.

Things were beginning to change. Finally, after so many years, the tides were shifting in my direction.

And I would do everything in my power to make sure things stayed that way.

My plans are finally about to come to fruition...

CHAPTER 21: QUESTIONS AND ANSWERS

HAEL

Our Rolls Royce drove through the Skeleton Quarter. Every inhabitant of this wretched place turned their heads in awe at the alien vehicle gracing their streets.

Loch and I were on a mission, and nothing would stop us.

Dane and Aneurin had poked the sleeping beasts. Stealing from Twin Leading Breeds would bring them nothing but pain and suffering.

They had taken something that was ours, and we would get it back.

Loch was resolved to make them pay, and I couldn't agree more.

In the past, we'd have simply flown out to the mountains and taught them another lesson. But after Zak left, Loch and I became more cautious. Who knew how many more dragons had joined them by now? We couldn't trust those vagrants to fight fairly.

The fact that Maddie had given them access to our residence was one thing. That she had allowed them to sneak out with Dragonstone was something far worse.

Loch and I still weren't sure how the twins were able to break in and take it. Req Tower was impenetrable. We had a state-of-the-art security system. Nothing and no one passed through our doors without us knowing.

How had they done it?

It was no matter. Two fucking druggies craving another fix would risk anything to get what they wanted. This risk, however, didn't warrant reward.

Quite the opposite, actually.

As for Maddie, she would have to pay for disappearing on us.

Since Loch had returned to his usual self, he'd been more willing to forgive some of the rat's minor indiscretions.

This time, he would not be so kind. And I wouldn't hold him back.

Our car finally came to a halt. We stepped out of the cool confines of our ride into the sweltering sun.

It was time to get some answers.

LOCH

The druggie ran as fast as his fucked-up legs could carry him.

It was no use. I barely had to exert any energy to keep up.

"It's no use, Kellen," I yelled. "You'll never get away."

"I didn't fucking do anything, man!" he replied breathlessly.

Hael and I knew this rodent from Club Emerald. He had caused trouble there on more than one occasion. We were merciful to him before, but if we didn't get any answers...

I relished in what we would do to his fragile little body.

"We just want to talk," I said.

"Fuck that! I know what kind of talking you do!"

If anyone had information on Dane and Aneurin, it was this fucking nobody.

It didn't escape our attention that he was also a dragon. Although, with all the drugs he'd taken, he was just a shell of his potential.

Maybe if he survived this interrogation, he'd make for an adequate addition to our horde...*never mind. Fuck that.*

Just when the little burnout thought he might have a chance to escape down a side alley, Hael was there to block his path.

With a simple shove, he flew into the nearest brick wall and collapsed to the ground.

"You didn't have to make it this hard," Hael said. "We only want answers."

"Well, I don't got any!" Kellen replied.

I stepped hard on his ankle. He screamed in agony.

"For your sake, you better hope you have answers," I sneered. "Tell us about the twins, Dane and Aneurin."

Kellen's eyes looked up in fright. It was obvious he knew the names, but I was interested in what else he might know.

"Please, my ankle," he squealed.

I relented and removed my foot. Kellen grabbed his ankle pitifully.

"Talk, weasel, or we'll rip that foot clean off your body," Hael growled.

"They're not here!" Kellen answered.

"We already know that!" I replied. "Tell us when they were last here."

"Dane and Aneurin haven't been in the Skeleton Quarter for weeks."

Hael and I shared a look.

Hael: Weeks? But we only noticed the missing Dragonstone recently.

Loch: He could be lying.

Hael: And if not? He knows what we'd do to him. I hate to admit, but this little scumbag might be telling the truth.

I grabbed the collar of his shirt in my hand and lifted him clear off the ground. His hands wrapped around mine, but he couldn't pry himself free.

"Tell us *everything* you know about them," I said, "or this will be your last fucking conversation."

"Once they left, they never came back. Not even to get a fix," Kellen stammered. "It's like they just went fucking survivor man or some shit."

"How many are with them?" demanded Hael.

"A lot," Kellen replied. "From the sound of it, they've got their own little village. A lot of other dragons have gone out there to learn from them."

"Have they asked you to join?" I asked.

"No, man. Dane and Aneurin only want clean dragons," he admitted. "I just can't quit overhead. You know?"

That meant their little commune had grown exponentially since Zak had left.

Not only that, but they were trying to strengthen the members of their pathetic little horde.

I'd heard enough.

I tossed Kellen to the side and listened as his hurried footsteps echoed down the alley.

Hael's eyes were piercing as they met mine.

If the twins hadn't stolen our Dragonstone, then that meant...

Loch: Do you know what this means, brother?

Hael: We've been after the wrong rat.

Loch: The brothers could have sent someone else to take the stone.

Hael: We both know that's not really possible. There's only one true culprit.

Loch: Indeed. And it's long past due for her punishment.

MADDIE

I looked out at the otherworldly terrain and was totally breathless.

The Dusk Mountains always made the faraway towers of Requiem City seem so small and insignificant.

Every time I'd visited Dane and Aneurin it was the same majestic feeling...as if there was magic pulsing through these mountains.

I never questioned why Dane and Aneurin would want to leave the hustle and bustle to try and find themselves in the wilderness.

I walked the narrow path over the rocks and through the trees. The rays of sunshine glistened through the leaves.

Up ahead, I heard voices and picked up my pace. That must be Dane and Aneurin!

As I pushed through the foliage and emerged into the large clearing, the sight surprised me.

It wasn't the voices of Dane and Aneurin.

There were *dozens* of people here!

I walked around the encampment and realized the faces were all watching me. Last time I'd been here, the twins were just getting things started.

I had just been impressed that they had a healing pool and a treasure cave.

But now they had their own small village!

I spotted Dane and Aneurin surrounded by what I could only

describe as groupies. Groupies! These guys were junkies only a few weeks before.

"Hello, there," said a female voice.

I turned to find a young woman smiling brightly at me. She wore a light cotton dress, and her hair was in braids. She looked dazzling.

"My name's Summer. It's nice to meet you."

She extended her hand, and I accepted her handshake.

"I'm Maddie. Nice to meet you too."

"*The* Maddie? Oh my gosh! Dane and Aneurin have told me so much about you," she said. "It's nice to see another friendly face at the commune."

She gave me a quick, unexpected hug. It felt weird to be so welcomed by a stranger.

Hell, at least she wasn't trying to kill me...

"How did you find out about this place?" I asked, still shocked.

"I can't really explain it," she admitted. "I met them one day in the emergency room. Dane was badly wounded. After I helped them...I just couldn't get them out of my head."

So *this* was Dane and Aneurin's new lady! I remembered them mentioning the cute nurse they had met after their fight with Loch and Hael.

Ugh. Loch and Hael.

Just thinking about them hurting Dane made my blood boil.

Summer continued. "They asked me to join them out here and I just said...well, what the heck!"

She motioned around the camp.

"Pretty impressive, isn't it?" she asked.

"Uh, yeah. It's fucking unbelievable," I replied. "Who are all these people? What are they doing here?"

Summer smiled at me but shook her head.

"It's kind of difficult to explain," she replied. "But I think they feel the same pull I did. Some desire to be out here with the twins."

"Not gonna lie, if I didn't have my own unexplained desires to stay in the Dobrzyckas' orbit, I'd be baffled too," I said.

Summer nodded in understanding.

"It's probably best to talk to the leaders themselves," she said.

Leaders?

"Oh God," I said. "Please don't tell me this is a cult."

She laughed loudly before taking my hand in hers. Together, we walked over to Dane and Aneurin.

The twins finally noticed my presence and beamed with joy.

"Maddie!" they shouted simultaneously.

"You finally made it back out here," Dane said, smiling. "What do you think?"

I took another look around.

"It's amazing," I said.

"It's a big improvement from last time," Aneurin added. "But it'll just keep getting bigger."

Finally, I found enough of my voice to speak.

"Is this your...horde?" I asked.

"You know it," Dane smiled.

Damn. It had grown exponentially in such a short time.

I looked at the two former druggies and felt a sense of pride. Loch and Hael were having trouble finding new dragons to join their horde, but Dane and Aneurin had followers without even trying.

It showed how true leaders should act: instead of putting people down, they should build them up.

Even though I was happy for Dane and Aneurin, I didn't totally understand why they were building a horde. What was it all for?

The twins noticed my confusion.

"You're probably wondering why we're building a horde," Aneurin stated.

"She was asking a lot of questions," Summer chimed in.

I nodded my head.

Yeah, and I want some damn answers!

"It might not make total sense," Dane began, "but it's just something we've been feeling."

"Ever since you helped us discover our real powers as dragons," Aneurin added, "we've had a nagging feeling that something is going to happen."

"Something bad?" I asked.

The twins nodded gravely. The smile on Summer's face faded.

"There's a war coming," Dane said solemnly. "We don't know how we know it...we just do."

This wasn't the first time I'd heard someone mention a war. My stomach began to twist into knots as I realized that if everyone could feel it coming...it must be real.

"Couldn't you lie and tell me you're feeling weird from eating some bad food?" I asked.

They didn't crack a smile. Instead, their faces grew even more severe.

"At first it was just Dane and me," Aneurin continued. "But we needed more. If there is something ominous on the horizon, we can't face it alone."

"Whatever's coming is bad, Maddie," Dane said. "Real bad."

Aneurin nodded his head. "And it could destroy everything that we've ever known."

CHAPTER 22: WAKING THE DEAD

ZAYDA

Another late night at the lab. It was becoming my daily routine: meet up with Xander at the laboratory to take blood, then go home feeling like a zombie.

Yesterday Xander had claimed that he'd taken all the blood he would need.

And I found that I didn't want to be home anymore.

There was really nothing else that occupied my attention from my own worst thoughts.

It was bad enough that my friendships had taken a hit in recent weeks. Sure, I still talked with Darshan and Thea. But it wasn't the same without Maddie, no matter how much she pissed me off.

Our lives were all on different trajectories, and the only one that seemed to get me was...

My stomach lurched at the recollection of Xythor.

All I wanted was to be held in his arms...to smell the sweet aroma of his body...to feel the soft touch of his lips...

I stood up from my station and thought about leaving. But where would I go? Back to an empty apartment, haunted by the ghosts of my memories?

It seemed better to be stuck in the depths of XU, consumed with work.

I'd finally gotten some energy back after feeling like a husk of a person after all the blood loss. With the prospect of another sleepless night looming, I decided to make my way to the lab.

Before heading to my workstation, I stopped by the kitchen. The lights flickered on, and I looked around at the empty table and chairs.

Apparently I was alone wherever I went—home or work.

I went to the coffee machine and turned it on. It buzzed to life as it warmed up the water and poured out a steaming stream of coffee.

I sipped the bitter liquid. It would taste better with some milk and sugar, but I was too damn tired to care.

The coffee moved slowly down my throat and into my stomach, warming my body. As I looked down the empty hall, I felt the sudden urge to explore.

It seemed no coincidence that the caffeine was already hitting me.

Instead of heading back to the laboratory, I walked in the other direction. It wasn't long ago I'd found a room with secret blueprints.

What other secrets could be hiding in these rooms?

I wandered down the halls, listening to my footsteps echo off the tile.

Turning a corner, I realized that I'd come to a dead end.

I was about to head back to the laboratory when a familiar jolt of electricity surged through my body.

Holy shit...

The energy reminded me of what I used to feel in the presence of Xythor.

I shook my head, trying to wake up my brain.

Maybe I did need to go home...or at least cut back on the caffeine.

I took another step and nearly stumbled. There it was again! That spark was unmistakable. But why was I feeling it now?

The hairs on my arms stood on end. They pointed in the direction of an unmarked door, like an explorer's compass pointing north.

I walked toward the unmarked door, and the gravitational pull grew stronger.

Something was behind that door...something strange and yet... familiar.

To my surprise, the door was unlocked. I turned the knob and pushed it open.

The lights flickered on. It took a moment for my eyes to adjust to the sight.

What the fuck is going on?

Before me, on a large metal table, lay Xythor's body. His face, chest, and arms were exposed, while the lower half of his body was covered with a white cloth.

I knew that Xander was bringing him back to life...but I had no idea he'd already finished.

Why hadn't he told me?

Xythor looked like the real thing. But it was hard to ignore the parts of his body that were covered with metal.

Something in my body told me to turn around and run...to get as far away from him as possible.

I just couldn't force myself to leave.

He was the Xythor I knew—the one I'd grown to love. There was no mistaking the familiar energy surrounding his body.

It was his face, the arch of his brow and the bones of his cheeks. Each muscle of his chiseled body was exactly what it'd been before.

When Xythor had died, his body was gaunt. His muscles rapidly deteriorated, leaving behind only skin and bones.

Metal coils wound around his arms and legs, reminiscent of the blueprints I'd seen days earlier. Was this to strengthen his frail remains?

Or did Xander intend to use Xythor as some sort of prototype for his robot army?

I moved forward and reached out my hand.

I flinched as I touched his cheek. It was surprisingly warm.

Suddenly, the table began to rumble, and I jumped back.

Then Xythor opened his eyes.

At first, I wanted to scream, but there was no voice in my throat. I backed up and bumped into the wall, watching in horror as Xythor sat up.

His head turned and looked at me.

"Zayda?" he said.

It was hard to believe, but it was his voice. And those were his blazing blue eyes that recognized me.

He held out his hand and waved me toward him. Should I believe what was happening? What if it was merely a dream, and I reached out only to wake up at my desk?

Xythor had died. I'd lain at his side as his heart had ceased beating in his chest. But Xander, a man I'd grown to hate, had kept his word.

Somehow, with my blood and the process of alchemy, Xythor was resurrected.

"Please," he said meekly, "don't be afraid."

I moved toward him and placed my hand in his.

"Xythor," I said. "Is it really you?"

He wrapped his arms around my waist and pulled me closer. I reveled in the sudden burst of energy transferred between our bodies.

I'd thought I'd never feel this way again. And yet, it was happening!

"Who else could it be?" he asked.

I didn't know the answer to that, and I didn't want to know.

My hands touched his face, feeling every contour of his jaw. His blue eyes were still staring at me, and I couldn't help but notice the confusion.

He was just as lost as I was.

I bent down and kissed his lips, unable to stop the desire growing in my body. I'd spent too many nights longing for my man. And here he was in the flesh...and metal...

My hands ran down his bulging biceps and touched bits of cold metal. Contrasted with the warm skin, it shot bolts of chilled passion through me.

I removed the cloth covering the lower part of his body and gasped at the sight.

His cock was growing erect before my eyes. Somehow, it seemed bigger than it was before.

It just. Kept. Growing.

I touched his tip and gasped with pleasure. He rubbed my ass and squeezed gently.

I couldn't deny this carnal passion anymore. I quickly unbuttoned my pants and kicked them off—my panties were next.

Xythor couldn't wait any longer. He grasped my shirt in both hands and with a firm tug, split it down the middle, ripping it off my body.

I unfastened my bra and let it fall away. The cold air of the room instantly made my nipples hard.

Xythor leaned forward and licked each breast. Shivers went up and down my spine as his warm tongue lapped at my skin.

I felt his heavy hand touch my legs, and I moved them apart. His finger rubbed against the crease of my pussy, stroking me softly.

I kissed him hard, our tongues dancing madly.

His finger slipped inside me, and I moaned with ecstasy.

Who knew that a robot's finger could feel so damn good? I grasped his hand with my own and held it firmly against my clit while his finger fucked me into a near orgasm.

This was it...everything I'd been wanting—found right here in the depths of this godforsaken university.

Wasting no more time, Xythor grabbed my waist and lifted me up in the air, setting me down on top of his throbbing cock.

"Holy fucking shit!"

My body shook with unbelievable rapture as I felt every inch of his gigantic erection.

I looked into his eyes as I kept sliding down, wondering if I would ever reach the end of his shaft.

I finally stopped at the hilt of his dick but wanted more. I wrapped my arms around his shoulders and pushed myself tighter against him.

"Jesus fuck, I'm gonna cum!" I cried out.

Xythor's hips rocked back and forth in gentle motions. He was sitting, holding my quivering body as his pulsing dick seemed to venture all the way up into my stomach.

It feels so damn good.

My grip grew tighter and tighter as I continued to bear hug Xythor. He didn't seem to mind, and in return, his hands wrapped firmly around my ass.

He pushed and pulled as his hips continued to gyrate. My legs dangled off the sides of the table and gravity kicked in, pressing me tighter against my man.

I felt as if I'd reached some type of blissful state only experienced by disciplined monks in remote mountain monasteries.

Tears streamed down my cheeks as I continued to cum over and over, soaking the table with my juices.

He came inside me, and I felt every burst of hot, sticky seed. It was as if a cannon had been released in my belly.

Finally, slowly, I stood up off his redwood cock. I lay down on the table beside him.

I looked into his beautiful blue eyes and wanted to tell him everything I was feeling. He was my one true love, and this was my second chance. I couldn't let him leave me again.

But if I told him everything—that would mean explaining the child growing inside.

Was I ready for his reaction so soon after we had been reunited?

If I didn't tell him now, I wasn't sure when I'd get another chance.

"Xythor," I whispered, "I have to tell you something."

"What is it?" he asked, kissing my cheek.

"I didn't think I'd ever get you back."

I burst into uncontrollable tears, overwhelmed by the realization that I actually had my man back.

Xythor embraced me in an unbreakable bear hug. I never wanted to leave his arms.

"I'm here," Xythor said. "And I'm never going anywhere again."

"Do you mean it?" I asked.

"Of course," he replied. "I would never lie to you."

More tears streamed down my cheeks. Xythor gently wiped them away. I couldn't hold back my secret any longer.

"I'm pregnant," I whispered.

Xythor smiled, and for the first time in days, I was whole.

I laid my head on his shoulder and stroked my hand down his chest. He kissed me on the forehead. I felt like a burden had been lifted off of my shoulders and tossed into the deepest ocean, never to return.

My eyes grew heavy with sleep, and within a few minutes, I could no longer hold them open.

The sun's orange glow bathed the clouds in the sky with its fiery light.

Wherever I was looked like a war zone.

Shattered glass and twisted metal from smashed cars littered the streets. I tried to find my way through the maze of destruction, but there was no safe path.

Every direction I looked was the same...nothing but ruin.

I tried to head toward a line of trees that outlined the beginning of the forest. The metal and glass crunched under my feet.

The closer I moved toward the trees, the worse it smelled. Burned hair and overcooked barbeque wafted in my nostrils.

I was unfortunate enough to look down and see the origin of the smells...charred bodies...dozens of them.

They were burned to blackened crisps.

I opened my mouth to scream, but my voice was drowned out by something else.

A roar rumbled from the sky, forcing my eyes to the now blood-red clouds.

Dragons soared high in the air, fighting with one another. After a few more moments, I realized that they weren't fighting among themselves, but with another foe.

As the dragons twisted and turned, I could see metal glinting in the dying rays of the sun.

Robots! The dragons were fighting robots!

The two enemies took a nosedive toward the ground. I gasped as green, red, and blue fire erupted from their mouths.

Everything in their paths exploded with the unbelievable heat of their flames.

And then the dragons and robots turned toward me.

I looked around once more but was racked with fear. There was nowhere to hide.

Soon, I would be just like the bodies beneath my feet...a lump of charcoal...another victim to the war of the dragons...

CHAPTER 23: BATTLE ON THE MOUNTAIN

LOCH

Our wings blotted out the sun, casting giant shadows over the treetops. Each flap of our wings sent a flurry of wind, which shook the leaves, even though they were several hundred feet below.

Hael and I were nearing the Dusk Mountains and our subsequent reunion with Dane and Aneurin.

We'd been here once before and had left as victors. If we had our way, this time we would wipe them from the face of this earth.

This wasn't something we wanted to do. It was a necessity.

We needed to find Maddie and try to retrieve the Dragonstone before it fell into the wrong hands.

It was just our luck that Maddie had been relying more and more on wearing her mint bracelet. We didn't know if they'd spoken to her recently.

But these punk twins were our only hope of finding her.

Hael: I see something in the distance.

Loch: Is it the twins?

Hael: Yes, and many more.
It looks like an encampment.

Loch: Their horde?

Hael: That's entirely possible.

Loch: Let's make our descent.

Hael and I drifted through the air until our massive talons dug into the soft mountain dirt. We shifted into our human forms, black leather pants and all.

There was no telling what to expect, arriving at the Dusk camp. One thing was sure—we weren't going to let them take us by surprise.

We began walking a narrow dirt trail toward the encampment.

Their setup was impressive, even for two lowlifes. Tents were set up for their followers, and a wooden platform held a couch and chairs. In the distance, hammocks stretched from tree to tree, made with vibrantly-colored fabric.

"Do you think she's here?" Hael asked.

I sniffed the air and smelled moisture. There was a storm in the distance, but we still had plenty of time to take care of business before it hit.

"For the sake of all dragons, let's hope so," I said. "If not, maybe they've talked to her."

"If she went to them, I'll be pissed," Hael said. "We're her mates. To think that she would bypass her fated bond and seek comfort in other dragons!"

I watched as his nostrils flared with rage. Hael was ready for battle.

I hadn't seen him like this in years. And I had to admit, I was glad to see him so bothered by Maddie's choices.

We'd tolerated her bratty behavior for far too long.

If she did steal the Dragonstone, it was the last straw.

But her punishment wasn't what we needed to think about at the moment.

We needed to get that stone back before it was too late.

"I can't wait for the sunset," Maddie said. "I hope it's going to be as beautiful as last night's."

She was talking with a group of people, Dane and Aneurin among them. They had no idea we had entered their camp.

Their followers had spotted us as we entered from the trail and walked through the small village of tents. Most simply stared before going back to their own business. Others whispered with their neighbors, but no one impeded our path.

The place was littered with wildflowers, and a large stream babbled nearby. It was actually quite beautiful if one cared about such simple pleasures.

"Hopefully the incoming storm clouds won't block the view," a woman said.

"Yes, let's hope that's the case," Hael said sarcastically.

The group of people quickly turned to see who owned the unfamiliar voice.

I spotted our former protégé Zak, and we locked eyes.

I could sense his fear and uncertainty. If Hael and I hadn't had more important business, I'd have taught the young traitor a lesson he wouldn't soon forget.

Dane and Aneurin shot up from the stumps they sat on.

"What the hell are you doing here?" Dane asked.

"It looks like they've come looking for round two," Aneurin responded.

I looked at the twins before turning my attention to Maddie.

The little mouse was absolutely in shock at our appearance.

"We've come to talk with our mate," I replied. "If all goes accordingly, there won't be the need for another fight."

"You shouldn't be here at all," Aneurin growled. "So why don't you save yourselves the trouble and leave? *Now.*"

Hael chuckled at the weak threat.

These pieces of gutter trash hadn't even known their potential until our mate had found them. Did they seriously think we should feel threatened?

"You don't have to do this," Maddie said, angry. "You don't have to start a fight. I'll talk to you willingly."

"You'll do as we say," I retorted. "This isn't some game. Give us back the Dragonstone."

"It would be wise to listen," added Hael. "Your punishment will be less severe if you obey our commands."

"She's not doing anything," Dane shouted.

Another woman stepped forward. She seemed familiar, as if I'd passed her on the street.

She was beautiful in a way that reminded me of Maddie.

I shifted in place, uncomfortable with my thoughts about this woman.

She looked at us with annoyance but tried her best to win us over with a smile.

"I don't know what's happening," the woman said, "but can we take this somewhere more private?"

"Stand back, Summer," Aneurin called out. "You don't know what they're capable of."

Summer...

Where had I heard that name before?

I racked my brain, trying to figure out the answer, but Hael was obviously less concerned.

"Listen to them," Hael replied. "We've come for Maddie, and

we won't leave until we have her."

Dane and Aneurin ordered their followers into their tents.

They believed our threats but didn't seem afraid. Had they learned nothing from their previous defeat?

It was time to remind them what it's like to challenge Twin Leading Breeds.

The twins motioned to Maddie, and she followed them out of the camp and into a large clearing. I looked around, expecting some sort of trap, but there was none.

"If you want her," Dane said, "then you've got to go through us first."

Before I could even react, Hael had already misted into his full dragon form. One of us was enough to make any sane person go crazy.

But when we both shifted, we could cause full-blown bedlam.

I joined my brother and felt a significant strength surge through my body. This would be over shortly, but I would take my time ripping these punks limb from limb.

A sudden roar pierced the air, but it hadn't come from Hael or me.

It was the twins!

Their dragons had grown since our first battle, and their scales shined brighter in the sun.

This wouldn't be just another easy victory like I'd thought...

Perhaps we finally had a real battle on our hands.

Hael and I took off into the sky.

Dane and Aneurin were close behind.

MADDIE

Shit. This wasn't good.

I stared into the sky as the four massive dragons battled each other. The first blasts of fire had been brilliant, like fireworks on a hot summer night.

The terrible roars brought me back to reality. This wasn't some light show, it was a battle to the death.

"What the fuck is going on?" Summer screamed.

She stared in awe at the scene above us.

"They're battling...for me," I said.

Summer shook her head, lost in her own baffling thoughts.

"We've got to do something," she pleaded. "What if they get hurt? I've already saved them once. But this is...this is something else entirely."

She wasn't wrong. It would be hard for any person to comprehend such a sight for the first time. Though she had been able to save Dane before, after a similar battle.

But if Loch and Hael got what they really wanted, there would be nothing left of Dane and Aneurin but bloody skeletons.

"Dane! Aneurin! Stop this!" she screamed into the sky.

It was no use. They couldn't hear her even if they wanted to.

"I'm sorry this is happening," I said.

"If you're sorry, then do something," she replied, annoyed.

Fuck.

I tried to hum a tune, but the battle above kept distracting me from remembering the right melody. The songs I'd always sung to put them to sleep were somehow wiped from my memory.

Loch and Dane's dragons swooped down, their jaws snapping at each other's throats. Summer and I hit the deck as they flew dangerously close.

Hael and Aneurin's dragons were chasing one another high in the clouds. Green and gold spouts of fire lapped at their scales.

"You have to try and communicate with them," I said.

"How the hell can I do that?" she asked, confused.

That was a great question.

It had come so easily for me and the Dobrzyckas that it seemed like a bad joke trying to explain it to her.

"Well, I guess close your eyes," I began, "and try to talk to them with your thoughts."

"What?!" she shrieked.

"Believe me! Just do it," I said. "Try to get Dane and Aneurin to lure them closer."

"You want them closer?!" she said, flabbergasted.

I shot her a look, and she shrugged without saying another word.

I unclamped my mint bracelet and slid it into my pocket.

Maddie: Loch! Hael! Please stop! I want you to punish me. Not them!

Loch: Shut your mouth, little rat!

Maddie: I'll give you the Dragonstone. I'll stay locked in a cage as long as you want. Just end this madness!

Hael: It's far too late for that.

So much for trying to talk about our issues...

Summer would need to have more luck. But if this was her first time, I didn't have much hope.

A shout of surprised joy came from Summer's mouth.

"I think I spoke to them!" she said. "I don't know which one. But I could hear their voices in my head. How is that possible?"

This must mean that Summer was branded to the twins—but they didn't know it yet?

"Just plain luck," I lied.

It would be too hard to explain everything to her now, but I was sure she'd figure it out in her own time.

Surprisingly, the two smaller dragons began to swoop back toward us.

Loch and Hael, massive and intimidating, were right on their tails.

I sucked in a deep breath and focused my thoughts. It was now or never...

I could hear a faint melody begin to play in my head. With each passing second, the song swelled louder.

My voice was usually soft and took time to warm up, but now it was unbelievably loud. I sucked in another breath as the dragons flew terrifyingly close.

"Dark is the wind,

"When it blows through the cave,

"And the wolf gets the poor shepherd's flock..."

I saw Dane and Aneurin falter first. Then their dragon bodies grew limp and fell to the earth, colliding with the ground.

Next were Loch and Hael. They tried to fly up and out of the range of my song, but I refused to let them off so quickly.

"Loud is the blood,

"As it lands in the mud,

"When it spills from the red, cursed rock."

Loch and Hael's dragon forms stopped their ascent and fell to the ground like dead birds. Their collision was much louder and sent dirt and debris raining onto our heads.

"Holy shit," Summer stammered. "You did it!"

I looked at her with a smile and shook my head.

"No, *we* did it. You were able to use the mind-link to bring them closer."

Summer lunged forward and gave me a hug, taking me by surprise. It was nice to feel the kind embrace of another woman. It had been missing for far too long from my life.

But the embrace was quickly broken as we heard the groans of Dane and Aneurin.

The fight had left them bloodied and bruised.

I wondered what Loch and Hael might look like, but they were nowhere to be seen. They were no doubt embarrassed by their fall and had already made their way toward cover.

Once again, I'd shown my power to be too much for the Dobrzyckas. They wanted to dominate me at every turn, but I could overpower any form they became.

But that wasn't important now.

Summer would have to save Dane and Aneurin.

And I would need to go try to smooth things over with two Dragon Lords who were *not* happy with me.

My mind raced...

What type of punishment did they have in store?

CHAPTER 24: HEALING TOUCH

SUMMER

I watched Dane and Aneurin resting in their hammocks. They were recovering under a full moon, its soft glow shining down on their perfect figures.

The sunset had been beautiful, just like Maddie had hoped. She had wanted to stay the night and make sure everything was alright, but I had managed to talk her into going home.

Maddie was exhausted after singing her beautiful and eerie song. She didn't look any different, but I could tell she needed rest. After all, a nurse always knows what's best...

Maddie reluctantly left to catch up on some sleep at her apartment. She gave me her number in case anything happened. But as I looked at the two men, I knew they would be just fine in my hands.

I'd gone through my usual routine, conjuring the healing energy of the earth to heal their major wounds. Yet again they were in awe of my healing powers.

But this time, I decided to go above and beyond for the two Dragon Lords.

I went to my tent and prepared a natural salve made of plants and other herbs found on the mountain. With the mortar and pestle,

I managed to quickly mash up a balm that filled my nostrils with pleasant scents.

Luckily, I'd taken a few classes on natural remedies. It seemed unnecessary at first, but now I was glad that I learned more than just how to administer medicine made in a lab.

Finished with my concoction, I prepared a healthy broth and placed it over an open fire to warm it up.

I took the salve to the two resting men. They were both awake and turned to look at me. I could see their blazing eyes gleaming in the moonlight.

"You're still awake?" Dane asked.

"Of course," I replied. "I'm surprised the two of you haven't fallen asleep after your big battle."

Aneurin laughed. "Our minds are racing too much for that."

"Not to mention the leftover adrenaline," Dane added.

I pulled up a nearby chair and sat down.

"What ya got there?" Aneurin asked, amused.

"This is going to help your bodies heal," I said.

"We're kind of new to this," Dane replied, "but dragons can heal on their own."

I laughed at the comment.

"It's almost like you've forgotten how we first met," I said, teasing. "Prove to me all your wounds are healed."

Aneurin and Dane gave each other a look. It was clear they were still in pain but didn't want to admit it.

"Okay, fine," Aneurin said, chuckling. "We haven't reached our full potential. But one of these days, your medicine and healing powers won't be necessary."

"So I should just go back to my own business then?" I asked, acting like I would leave.

"No, please stay," Dane said.

"We're stubborn but not stupid," Aneurin added.

I scooted the chair closer and dug my fingers into the pungent balm. I started spreading it along Aneurin's hip, where a large bruise had formed.

He groaned from the pain as my fingers pressed into the black and blue of his skin.

"Why does it burn?" Aneurin asked.

"That means it's working." I smiled.

I spread it over a few more places and then moved on to my next victim. Dane seemed more than ready for the hands-on treatment.

"You're a miracle worker," Dane moaned. "What do we gotta do to get more massages like this?"

"Get into more fights," Aneurin replied.

"It's not a massage," I said. "And the more fights you get into, the less I'll be willing to help."

I finished rubbing in the last of the salve and poured them each a bowl of the broth. They both slurped greedily before I could even tell them to slow down.

"You two are insatiable," I mused.

They didn't disagree, and we sat in peaceful silence for several moments, listening to the crackle of the nearby campfire.

Dane and Aneurin looked at one another and nodded their heads, seeming to talk to one another without uttering a word.

In the past, I'd have felt awkward watching this. After the events of today, I knew it was highly likely they were communicating.

Finally, they turned their attention to me.

"We wanted to talk with you about something," Dane said.

"What is it?" I asked.

Aneurin took a deep breath before beginning.

"It wasn't a coincidence that we found you," Aneurin said. "We could have been seen by any nurse, but we found you."

"Our brains have a way of making uncertainties seem like fate," I replied.

"You know that's not true," Dane said. "You *spoke* to us today using your thoughts."

I shrugged, unsure of what to say.

"That's something we do," added Aneurin. "We've never met anyone who could do that besides us."

If it weren't for Maddie, I would have never discovered that ability.

"You were meant to be with us," Dane said.

I listened to his words and felt a warm sensation trickle through my stomach, moving toward my limbs.

There was something about these two men. After all, I'd moved all the way out into the mountains just to be with them.

"Don't you feel it too?" Aneurin asked.

"Yes," I said quickly. "I feel something. I don't know what it is. But I always want to be around you. It's as if..."

"We belong together," Dane said, finishing my thoughts.

"Please don't take this the wrong way," Aneurin continued, "but we think you're our mate."

I chuckled at the thought of such a naive thing...

Mates? Destined to be together from the moment we were born?

But as silly as it sounded, I couldn't deny that it felt right.

Together, the twins rose out of their hammocks and each reached out a hand. I held them as they led me to a secluded area.

We entered their cave of treasure, and I was overtaken with darkness.

They snapped their fingers and any feelings of uncertainty were quickly swept away as orange light from several torches illuminated the small grotto.

They had made this cave into their own lair. The gold and jewels were still there, but several heavy rugs were strewn across the floor, giving the stone ground a soft touch.

The torchlight caught the giant, uncut diamond suspended from the cave's ceiling. Usually uncut diamonds don't sparkle. But this one lit up like a disco ball, sending a million beams of colorful light dancing throughout the cave.

It was absolutely mesmerizing.

I was shocked by how comfy it felt.

We moved deeper into the cave before they came to a halt.

"We're still new at this," Dane admitted.

"But we think we know what we have to do," Aneurin said. "Is it alright if we brand you?"

I would be lying if I said a part of me wasn't sure. But I trusted the two men standing before me. I would do anything to be with them.

"Yes," I said. "I trust you."

They each held out their open hands. Green and orange fire danced along their palms.

"Now stand still," Dane said.

"This won't hurt," Aneurin added. "We don't think..."

I watched them move closer and touch the fire to my arms and chest.

My instincts told me to run, but I tried to take in deep, calming breaths. My heartbeat was going into overdrive, though.

I shut my eyes, expecting to feel the worst pain I'd ever known.

But nothing happened.

I opened my eyes and found myself completely naked. The fire had burned away my clothes, but my skin was untouched.

Except for...

What is that?

I noticed a new tattoo around my thigh. It seemed to pulse with an otherworldly glow.

"That's your brand," Dane said.

"It proves that we all belong together," Aneurin said.

I looked at the twins. I had almost forgotten that I was *naked!*

For a split second, I wanted to cover up.

I'd never been with two men at the same time and was uncertain about how they felt about my most private parts.

Past lovers had complimented my curvy body and considerable breasts, but Dane and Aneurin were different. Maybe I wasn't what they wanted or expected...

Those thoughts quickly faded as I watched the twins look at me with a mixture of lust and longing. Suddenly, I didn't care that I was naked. My awkwardness evaporated.

I was glad they could see the real me. Just as much as I wanted to see them...

"Are you just going to stand there or join me?" I asked with a smirk.

As if a switch had been flipped, Dane and Aneurin ripped off their clothes.

Oh, shit. I wasn't ready for this.

Their naked bodies glistened in the torchlight. It was hard to believe that two former junkies could look this fucking good. Then again, they were dragons.

My mouth watered as my eyes took in every inch of their chiseled frames. And their cocks...

I moved forward and touched their chests with my hands. My body shivered with delight, and they had yet to even touch me.

They both leaned down and kissed my neck.

Their gentle lips felt so good...I wanted to melt right then and there.

I pushed them away and lay down on the rugs, motioning for them to join me.

They hurriedly obliged.

I took their swollen members in my hands and could not believe their size. My fingers could barely wrap around them.

I slid Dane's cock into my mouth, listening as he moaned with pleasure. His tip was already wet, and I could taste his salty goodness on my tongue.

My attention turned to Aneurin, who was practically trembling with desire. His moan was even louder than his brothers, and I dampened just hearing it.

They pulled themselves out of my grasp and spread my legs.

"Now, it's your turn," Dane said.

"Lie back and relax," Aneurin added.

I did as I was told and felt the soft fur rug caress my skin.

Dane's lips kissed my thighs gently before eventually making his way down to my dripping pussy. His tongue lapped at my clit and I felt euphoric.

Aneurin wasn't one to be left out. His warm lips sucked all over my breasts.

Their shared touch was sending double the fire through my blood.

After several moments of enjoying my juicy sweetness, the brothers switched positions.

Aneurin was just as gentle, but there was an insatiable craving in the way he moved his tongue.

I grabbed his head in my hands and pressed him tighter against my mound while Dane's lips alternated between my nipples.

I was unable to hold it back any longer.

I groaned in ecstasy as I came in Aneurin's face. He happily licked up the mess, thirsty for me.

"Fuck me," I whispered softly. "I want both of you... I can't take it anymore..."

Aneurin was already there, so he slid inside. There was a shock of pain from his girth, but it was quickly replaced by unbelievable euphoria.

I couldn't hold back my groans, so I grabbed Dane's cock and thrust it into my mouth. Aneurin lifted my legs over his shoulders and lifted me off the rug, pushing inside me with slow movements.

My legs trembled as I quickly reached another climax. How could I not? He was *so* damn huge!

It was apparent he wasn't used to something so tight because within minutes he shot his load inside me. The surge alone from his steady stream of cum caused me to climax with him.

Then it was Dane's turn.

I was still trembling from my last climax when his anaconda slithered inside. My body twitched and shook as he pushed all the way to the base of his shaft.

I licked the tip of Aneurin's still-throbbing dick, tasting his salty goodness mixed with my sweet pussy juices.

Dane thrust harder than his brother, but I didn't feel any pain. The only sensation I felt was my eyes rolling back in my skull as I released another earthquake of an orgasm.

My pussy's convulsions gripped Dane's thrusting cock even tighter. There was no way he could hold on as I bucked my hips.

Dane lasted for several more seconds until he could take no more. He pulled out his cock and shot his hot load all over my stomach and chest.

Finally spent, the twins laid on either side of me while I caught my breath. They gently rubbed their hands on my pussy, massaging it with careful caresses.

For several minutes, small aftershocks continued to rock my body.

"I've never felt that way in my entire life," I admitted. "You took me to heaven."

They took turns kissing my lips.

I savored the smell of our sex.

"We've never felt that way either," they said simultaneously.

"You're our mate," Aneurin said. "This is what it should feel like every time we're together."

"We're in love with you. We want to worship you every moment of every day," added Dane.

And they could do it. If sex with them felt this amazing, they could worship me until the end of time.

CHAPTER 25: WEDDING DAY!

MADDIE

I looked at my dress in the mirror, admiring the way it hugged my curves. It had been a long, restless night at the penthouse after yesterday's fight. To my surprise, things had actually started to get back on track.

Loch and Hael had tried to completely destroy Dane and Aneurin. Luckily, I found my voice just in time to stop my mates from getting their way.

When we arrived back at the penthouse, they were too exhausted from their battle to punish me right away.

They were still pissed about the Dragonstone. But we eventually came to an agreement.

I promised them I would submit to *any* punishment they saw fit...

If they behaved as my plus-twos to Darshan and Thea's wedding.

Of course, they didn't have to agree. But we all had so much more fun when I was a willing sub.

As I continued to admire my dress, Loch entered the room wearing only his leather pants.

It took me a few moments to rip my eyes away from his chiseled abs.

"You'd better get ready!" I said. "The wedding's only a few hours away."

"I hate weddings," Loch growled. "Can't we just stay in for the day? After all, we still haven't punished you yet."

He spanked my ass hard. I glared at him in the mirror, trying not to let him see how much the sting actually turned me on.

"You'll get your chance to discipline me," I teased. "But only if you make good on your side of the bargain."

"We're Twin Leading Breeds," Hael said, entering the room. "*You* submit to *our* needs."

Hael was dressed just like Loch, in nothing but leather pants. I was getting annoyed at how fucking delicious they looked.

Hael moved closer and bit my shoulder, sending shivers down my spine.

"I can't wait for this fucking day to be over," Hael grinned. "Oh, the things we've got planned."

More shivers went through my body. It was hard to stop myself from tearing off the dress and letting them take me.

I took in a deep breath and steeled my nerves.

"Get your suits on!" I demanded. "These are my best friends. We can't be late!"

Loch and Hael grumbled as they made their way toward the closet.

I smiled. They drove me crazy, but I wouldn't have it any other way. At least they weren't causing trouble. Today was *not* the day.

As soon as I saw Thea in her dress, everything sank in.

My best friends' big day was finally upon us.

Thea couldn't have looked more beautiful.

I'd expected to be a part of the procession. I hadn't seen her much lately, so I thought maybe I would only get to be a bridesmaid.

So when she'd asked me to be her Maid of Honor, I was blown away.

Then again, I *was* one of her best friends...

Her *other* best friend was in the room with me, looking at the bride-to-be as she held back tears.

My friendship with Zayda was almost non-existent. We weren't just on shaky ground—it was as if a fault had split open between us.

But weddings seemed to bring everyone together. I had to at least try and show some kindness toward my former friend. No matter how I felt about her recent choices.

Even though we hadn't really talked with one another, we were still as cordial as we needed to make Thea's day one she wouldn't forget.

"You look gorgeous," Zayda said to her.

"Agreed one million times over," I added.

Thea's face scrunched up once more as she tried to keep it together. It wouldn't do if the bride had mascara stains down her cheeks and on her white dress.

"Do you really think so?" she asked.

Zayda and I nodded vigorously.

Of course we did.

Thea's dress perfectly accentuated every curve on her rock-hard body. Hell, looking at her made me jealous, and I didn't even want to get married!

It wasn't just Thea who looked amazing. Everything for this wedding had been planned and executed to perfection.

Of course it helped that Thea and Darshan had well-paying jobs at a top-tier restaurant. But they had worked extra hard to make sure that nothing was out of place.

"You look like an angel," Darshan's voice called out.

All three of us turned in horror. Low and behold, the groom-to-be was standing in the doorway with a massive smile on his face.

Zayda and I instinctually formed a barrier to block his view.

"Darshan!" I yelled. "You're not supposed to be here!"

"It's bad luck," Zayda added.

"Oh, come on!" he retorted. "It's not like I can actually see anything."

That didn't matter. Rituals were not going to be broken today!

"Stay here," I said to Zayda. "I'll take care of this."

I hooked Darshan's hand in my own and walked him out into the hallway.

"She looks beautiful, though, right?" he asked.

"Absolutely," I replied. "And so do you."

I stood on the stage in awe at the ceremony around me.

Darshan and Thea had somehow managed to rent out a majestic old church that always seemed to be booked.

The building itself was a sight to behold with its high ceilings, gothic arches, and mahogany pews. The touches added for the wedding had taken it to a whole other level.

Garlands of white and blue flowers lined the balcony encircling the inside of the chapel.

Warm summer sunlight sifted through stained glass windows, washing the interior in a kaleidoscope of colors.

I looked out at the mass of bodies lining the pews and chairs, unable to believe that Darshan and Thea knew so many people.

The music suddenly swelled, and Thea made her way down the aisle, accompanied by her father.

Oohs and ahhs echoed throughout the church as everyone watched the gorgeous bride make her way to the altar.

Darshan was already waiting with a smile that no one could ever wipe away. Harry was his best man, and he nodded at me from across the stage.

This was really happening!

Thea arrived and stood next to her soon-to-be husband. It was impossible to hold back my tears, and I let them flow freely down my cheeks.

The officiant began the ceremony, but I couldn't focus on his words.

Seeing my two best friends about to pledge their lives to each other was sending me into a minor existential crisis.

Would I have to marry Loch and Hael one day? Why hadn't they proposed yet? Was I beneath them even in that regard?

Being branded by the Dobrzyckas was both a blessing and a curse.

It showed me a world that people only saw in movies: lavish penthouses, the finest foods, and designer clothes I'd only ever dreamed of wearing.

What would my life look like if I'd never stolen from the Dobrzycka family? Every time I was around them, my heart went into overdrive. It was impossible to keep my cool around my mates.

They had me in the palms of their hands, even if sometimes I wondered what it would be like to be free. Not necessarily from them but from every god damn thing that had happened in my life that just felt totally out of my control. I was always thrust into trouble. Why did it seem like everyone else had it so easy?

I was torn from my moment of self-pity as Thea gestured for the wedding band. I handed it over. She slipped it on Darshan's finger, and they shared their first kiss as a married couple.

Then I realized...maybe I was just jealous of their wedding. Fuck my feelings, they made no sense. It was just one big chaotic mess... but I guess I did love to fuck everything up in my *own* life. Maybe I was just addicted to trouble.

The applause was deafening, and not a single eye in the entire chapel was dry.

Regardless of my inner turmoil, I was so happy for my friends and the new life they had together.

But I couldn't stop thinking...what would be different if I'd never been born in Requiem City?

While the ceremony was a pleasantly subdued and thoughtful affair, the reception turned everything up to eleven.

I'd barely managed to change into a more casual dress when the band started the first of many sets.

After all the tears were wiped away, people were all smiles and ready to party.

I made my way to the open bar and ordered a gin and tonic. I looked at the back of the churchyard and found myself in awe.

There was a large patio on which a big table and chairs had been set up for dinner. A short way past that was a dance floor and small stage where the band played rocking covers of all our favorite songs.

At the very end of the stage was a yard adorned with beautiful, manicured foliage that looked like something out of a fairytale.

I sipped on my cocktail and admired the unbelievably perfect day. Not a cloud hung in the sky, and for once the sunshine wasn't overwhelming.

Let's just hope it would stay this way...

I felt a familiar burn on my shoulder. It was my brand.

Loch and Hael were nearby.

When we had first arrived at the wedding, I'd had to attend to my duties as Maid of Honor. Loch and Hael had promised to be on their best behavior when we parted ways.

I could only hope they had kept their promise.

It didn't take long to pick them out of the crowd—they stood head and shoulders above everyone else. Of course they were walking right toward me.

"Did we tell you how perfectly delectable you look, little mouse?" Hael asked, eyeing me up and down.

I tried not to blush, but it was impossible. I couldn't deny that my dress did look damn good on me.

"You two don't look so bad either," I replied.

They were both dressed in matching black suits. Loch had chosen the all-black look, while Hael had added some color to his attire with a dark green tie that complimented his hair color.

On anyone else, it might have looked stupid, but they knew how to wear suits like no other men...or dragons, for that matter.

"It was actually quite a nice ceremony," Loch said. "Thank you for the invitation."

I nearly choked on my cocktail hearing these words from Loch's mouth. It wasn't like him to be satisfied with anything except his own wealth and good looks.

"Well, you were my plus-twos," I replied, flabbergasted. "I'm glad you decided to attend."

"We haven't seen you for a while," Hael admitted. "It was starting to get unbearable."

"It's barely been an hour!" I exclaimed.

"And that's too long," Loch said with a smirk.

My brand burned hotter than it had in a very long time. I wanted to grab both of their hands and take them to the confessional booth. I had a lot of repenting to do, and Loch and Hael could definitely teach me a thing or two about reaching a higher power...

It took every ounce of energy for me to hold back my desire.

Not at a wedding, Maddie!

Zayda slid in beside me at the bar and ordered a Virgin Manhattan.

It was normally a stiff drink, but this one was made with several different types of juice. Hell, after everything she'd been through, I wouldn't blame her if she ordered an actual cocktail.

She smiled at me and then turned to Loch and Hael.

"Gentlemen," she said.

"It's wonderful to see you," Hael replied.

"If you'll excuse us, dinner is about to be served. And I must admit, I'm famished," Loch said dryly.

The twins walked away, and I shook my head with annoyance.

"God, they know how to ruin a moment," I said.

Zayda laughed at my joke. She held out her glass, and we did a short toast before we each downed our drinks in one gulp.

I looked into her eyes and felt a spark of the friendship we once had. It was still there, buried under layers of sediment and unnecessary bad blood.

I wanted to apologize and try to get our friendship back on track. But when I opened my mouth, the words that came out were completely unexpected.

"Shit's been so crazy lately," I blurted.

Zayda was taken aback.

"Yeah," she replied. "And why do you think that is?"

I saw the annoyed look on her face and realized I'd walked right into a hornet's nest.

"Well, I guess it's a number of things," I answered.

"And they're all my fault, right?"

Her eyes burned with resentment.

"No, not entirely," I admitted.

"What a fucking relief," she said. "It's nice to know you might take *some* of the blame for once."

"Sure, I'll take some of the blame," I retorted. "Only when you admit that Xander has you completely mind-fucked!"

Zayda took in a deep breath. She was so angry I could nearly feel the heat radiating from her body.

How had this conversation gotten out of hand so quickly?

I searched my mind for some way to end this stupid argument, but I had nothing. Not even our best friend's wedding could save our relationship now.

Then we heard the screams.

At first, it sounded like an overzealous attendee.

But as I watched people hurriedly moving away from the patio, I realized something was wrong.

A figure fell from the sky and touched down in the middle of the reception. Metal wings glistened in the sun. The body was made of half metal and skin, like something out of a sci-fi movie.

He had blue-black hair, a chiseled chest, and an unusually handsome face...

"Xythor?!" Zayda shouted. "But how is he here?"

That was a damn good question.

She looked at me with equal parts confusion and embarrassment. It sure was a surprise to see a dead man crash a wedding reception.

Zayda had told me that Xander had plans of resurrecting Xythor, but I thought it was just another one of my father's bullshit schemes.

But why was Zayda's undead boyfriend crashing our best friends' wedding?

"What the fuck is going on?" I asked.

"I don't know," she replied. "I thought I left him locked up in the lab..."

Her voice trailed off as she realized she'd said too much.

"He escaped Xander's lab?" I asked, pointing to the abomination on the patio.

She opened her mouth to answer, but it was too late.

A giant roar echoed throughout the church grounds, shaking the concrete beneath our feet.

I saw Xythor charging two figures, and my throat dropped all the way into my stomach.

It was Loch and Hael. With two puffs of smoke, they'd transformed into their dragon forms.

An all-out battle was about to begin.

CHAPTER 26: CAKE, DANCING & DRAGON FIRE

MADDIE

It was pandemonium. In the blink of an eye, a beautiful wedding gave way to fear and destruction.

Threatened by the presence of Xythor, Loch and Hael burst from their tuxes and morphed into dragons. Anyone who had never witnessed such a scene had no doubt gotten one hell of a show.

Those who didn't believe dragons existed were quickly thrust into a reality their minds most likely couldn't comprehend.

Me, I'd seen my fair share of dragon battles...

I was fucking pissed one was happening at my friends' wedding!

Loch and Hael soared high above the church, blotting out the sun's rays. They cast demonic shadows on the patio.

But it was their opponent that had me genuinely confounded.

Xythor soared along with them. His metallic body darted around the sky quicker than any dragon I'd ever seen.

The Dobrzycka dragons shot bursts of green and black flame that surrounded Xythor. But every time he emerged unscathed and retaliated with a fire blast of his own.

The golden fire that shot from his gaping mouth was as bright as the sun.

I shielded my eyes as the three dragons released simultaneous blasts. Their heat radiated all the way to the patio. Thea's dad's shoes melted right to the dance floor!

How the hell was I going to stop this?

I looked at Zayda, watching the battle next to me.

"What in the fuck is going on?" I demanded.

Zayda shook her head, still trying to gather all her thoughts.

"I don't know," she replied.

"Don't lie to me!" I yelled. "We have to stop this, or hundreds of people could be seriously hurt!"

Zayda's eyes met mine, and she nodded her head, understanding the severity of our situation.

"Tell me everything you know," I said.

"I left Xythor in the laboratory at Xander U," she admitted. "He must have broken out."

Or *someone* let him out...

Son of a bitch.

Was that why Xander wanted the Dragonstone? So he could bring a dead dragon back to life?

None of the answers mattered if we didn't stop the battle.

Zayda and I fell to our stomachs as Xythor zoomed overhead. Loch and Hael followed close behind. They flew so close I could've reached up and touched Hael's green scales.

Another spout of fire burned a section of tables filled with food trays and chocolate fountains. It went up in a burst of green flame, sending shrieks from nearby attendees.

I got to my feet and sprinted to the middle of the patio, which was littered with debris.

Loch and Hael were double-teaming Xythor, their jaws snapping at his metallic hide.

He fought back, ripping a chunk out of the side of Hael's green dragon.

I watched in horror as blood gushed from the wound, raining down on deckchairs below.

This battle was turning into a bloodbath—one my mates might lose!

"Xythor!" Zayda screamed. "Stop! There's no reason for any of this!"

Zayda could try to talk sense to a robot all day long but straining her voice would be the only thing she'd accomplish.

I remembered how I'd stopped the last dragon battle I'd seen. But if my voice wasn't loud enough to reach the dragons, it would do no good. My mates wouldn't listen to me, and who knew if robot Xythor could hear anything.

I looked around, feeling defeated and overwhelmed by the moment. People were crying on the steps of the church. Others crawled along the ground, the wounded bystanders of the raging battle.

It was too late to stop the fight. People's lives were already at stake because I didn't have any control over my mates.

I found my way to the stage the band had long since evacuated. The speakers were destroyed, so there was no use in trying the mic.

That didn't matter. I could at least channel my voice toward the sky and hope for the best.

We'd already seen the worst.

I recalled the words to the song and felt my body swell with newfound energy.

The haunting melody played loudly in my head.

My mouth opened, and my voice belted from my throat, filling the air with Freesia's ghostly tune.

But something was off...

It was almost as if my single voice had split into two...

I looked around as I sang the lyrics and couldn't believe my eyes.

Zayda stood on the ground beside the stage, belting the lyrics to the song word-for-word.

Holy shit!

She moved on to the third verse, and I quickly caught up, still unsure of how the hell she knew these words.

"I hear with my heart

"Your small ghost in the dark

"Now my curse is lain on the ground.

"My bonds have been broken

"The dark fate has spoken

"His black fire can't reach you now..."

As we finished the lyrics, my body felt alive with power. I'd never felt this way before.

I began to tremble. My lips stopped moving, effectively ending my part in the song.

My body felt different—more powerful. It was as if, by joining voices with Zayda, I'd been able to somehow absorb the powers of my mates...

When it seemed like my body couldn't handle the tremors, I raised my fists to the air and let out a hellacious scream.

The fire erupted from my fists, blasting toward the three dragons. Unaware of the incoming flame, all three were taken by surprise.

Hael and Loch took the brunt of the damage. Their wings went limp, and their bodies collapsed to the ground with a deafening crash.

Xythor was also hit by the blast, but his metal body repelled more of the damage than my mates.

Injured, but still airborne, Xythor spun away from the church and flew off into the horizon.

The song was finished, and the dragons were no longer fighting.

Now all I could hear were the screams of the remaining wedding guests.

I jumped down from the stage and ran toward the body of a young woman. She was conscious and breathing but looked to be in complete shock.

I ripped a part of cloth from my dress and wiped the blood and dirt from her body.

"It's okay," I said calmly. "Everything will be okay."

She nodded her head in understanding, but her body still shook from fear.

I quickly ran to the bar and grabbed a bottle of water before returning to the injured woman.

I noticed Zayda across the patio, helping someone who looked to have sustained a concussion.

She felt my gaze and looked in my direction. Her eyes were alive with a fire I'd never seen before.

How did she know the song?

It had come to me in a vision. The words were so powerful I'd never needed to write them down. There was no way she could have learned it from me without my knowing.

Then I remembered what Storm had once said: that one of my friends was unbelievably powerful and held the key to ending the impending war.

Singing together had unlocked something inside me that I never knew I possessed.

For some reason that made me more worried than excited.

If I had these powers, that meant Zayda could have them as well...

Was it possible we were *both* the second coming of Freesia?

STORM

I stood on the tallest peak of the Dusk Mountains with Silver at my side. In the distance, the robot dragon glided through the sky.

We had watched the dragon battle in silence. It was a sight to behold, but things got really interesting when the Dobrzyckas were knocked from the sky.

It was all beginning to come true. The revelations I'd had in the

Shadow Realm were manifesting in the outside world.

Requiem City would soon find itself in the crosshairs of a battle between dragon and man. Good and evil.

Which side would prevail? Which party would be exposed as the real evil?

"It's all coming to fruition," Silver said. "Your visions haven't let us down."

"Not yet," I replied. "There is still more than enough time to be proven wrong."

She nodded her head slowly, pained by the idea of false perception.

"We need to have a meeting," I said. "And it is in every dragon's best interest to attend."

Silver grabbed my hand and squeezed hard. Her touch gave me the strength that I hadn't realized I needed.

I closed my eyes and focused my thoughts.

Storm: Dragons. Friends. Enemies. The time is now.

Storm: A new enemy threatens to wipe us from the earth.

Storm: We need to discuss the future of our kind.

Storm: Gather your hordes and meet me at the Dusk Mountains.

Storm: War is upon us.

CHAPTER 27: A GATHERING STORM

STORM

The dragons descended from the sky and gathered on the peak of the mountain. It was a glorious sight to behold. It had been centuries since so many dragons had gathered together in one place.

But the reason for our gathering was not one of exaltation. There was a battle looming on the horizon like an approaching gale.

I surveyed the massive figures and was surprised by how many had heeded my call. Both the Dusk and Requiem hordes were present.

I knew the Dobrzyckas were having trouble finding other dragons, but there were more young dragons in their horde than I had expected.

Loch and Hael would be hard to convince. I knew they wouldn't be happy to band together.

For all I knew, Dane and Aneurin were just as likely to reject this alliance. But if dragons were to survive, joining forces was necessary.

Maddie and a young woman I'd met centuries ago, Summer, made their way toward me.

"Maddie, Summer," I said, welcoming them to the meeting.

Summer looked at Maddie cautiously.

"How do you know my name?"

"He knows a lot of mysterious shit," Maddie said. "I find it helps to just go along with it."

I laughed at her explanation.

"My name is Storm," I replied. "This is my mate Silver. We've been waiting

a long time to see you again."

Summer looked again at Maddie, who simply shook her head.

"He said the same shit to me," she said.

Summer shook off the confusion.

"Dane and Aneurin want to make sure this isn't some trick," she said. "They've already tussled one too many times with the Dobrzyckas."

"Tell them there is no need to worry," I assured her. "Our time together is too important for petty fighting."

Summer and Maddie both turned to their own hordes.

Upon realizing this wasn't some trick, Dane and Aneurin changed into their human forms. One by one, their horde followed suit.

It took the Requiem horde a bit more time to let down their guard.

Silver looked at me with a smile on her face. My visions were starting to come true.

We needed to make sure it stayed that way.

"Thank you all for coming," I said. "I know it is difficult to put aside your differences to assemble like this."

"Cut the small talk," Loch growled. "Why did you call us together?"

"Because the time to join hordes has never been more necessary than it is right now," I replied.

The Dobrzyckas laughed.

Dane and Aneurin responded with angry glares.

"We're not teaming up with these assholes," Dane said.

"Oh, but you're wrong," I replied. "The signs are all around us.

And more signals are showing up every day."

"What signs are you talking about, old man?" spat Hael.

I felt a tinge of anger at his remarks but shook them away.

"For one, Freesia's Rock is gushing blood," I responded. "Enough blood to spill out of the chapel giving it shelter."

My revelation wasn't scoffed at. Both hordes remained quiet.

"Secondly, that metal dragon you fought," I said, looking at Loch and Hael. "That could not have been possible without special means."

"What special means?" Loch asked.

"Dragonstone," I replied.

The Twin Leading Breeds looked at Maddie with utter contempt. She had been the one to give Xander the Dragonstone.

I had seen as much in my visions, but it was not entirely her fault. It was a necessary evil to jumpstart the war and bring the hordes together.

"That is not the problem, though," I assured them. "Freesia's curse seems to be getting stronger and shows no signs of weakening."

"We've been stuck here our whole lives," Hael said. "What do you expect us to do about it now?"

"Not just you," I smirked. "All of us."

The two hordes broke out into murmurs as they discussed the news.

I looked at Silver, and she nodded her approval. It was always good to have her by my side. She was the one who truly gave me hope for our future.

I grabbed her hand and squeezed it gently.

"Why should we join with another horde?" Loch asked. "We've been on our own for years. We've taken over Requiem City."

"There are no benefits to joining a couple of drug-addled dragons," added Hael.

Dane and Aneurin scoffed at the jab.

"We don't want to join a couple of uptight pricks," Dane snarled.

"You think you can take whatever you want," Aneurin said. "There's nothing I could respect about two megalomaniacs."

"Even your mate wants to leave you," Dane added.

Loch and Hael were set off by these words and started moving toward the other twins.

I rushed to put myself between them. Our world was indeed in danger if such trivial talk brought us down before we had even begun negotiations.

"You're blinded by your hatred!" I yelled. "Requiem City is a trap. Freesia's Curse has kept us here for centuries. As dragons, we're meant to roam skies the world over."

Loch and Hael looked at one another. The brothers knew I was right, even if they hated to admit it.

"I did almost lose Loch," Hael admitted. "It's in his blood to roam, and because he couldn't, he nearly set the city on fire."

I nodded my head without giving away my secret. It was because of me that Loch had gone crazy, but it had been necessary to test Maddie's power.

It was better that Loch and Hael didn't know the truth.

Dane and Aneurin nodded their heads in agreement.

"If it weren't for these mountains, we'd have gone crazy ourselves," Dane replied.

"We are meant to stretch our wings, to fly to the ends of this earth," I said. "You may own this city. But if we don't work together, we can never escape."

"What do we do?" Aneurin asked.

"Join forces," Silver said. "Or else die alone."

The two sets of twins looked at her with ponderous faces. They knew we had no reason to lie. But that didn't mean they would ultimately agree to our terms.

"Give us time to think," Loch said.

"The decision must be made today," I responded.

"We need time as well," Dane said, "but we'll give you an answer soon."

I watched the twins return to their hordes and speak with their groups. It was no longer up to me now.

Silver grabbed my hand once more.

"They will see the light," she said sweetly.

I hoped she was right.

MADDIE

While my mates discussed their decision among themselves, I gave them space. I headed toward Storm and Silver, who watched the two hordes with great interest.

It's now or never...

Storm and Silver seemed deep in thought as I approached. They turned to offer me smiles.

I was once again mesmerized by the golden glow in Storm's sunlike eyes.

"I would like to speak with you," I said meekly.

"Very well," Storm replied. "What is weighing on your mind?"

It was hard for me to find the proper words. He'd told me so much in our short meetings together.

"You once told me that I had a hand in ending the war," I said.

"That is correct," Storm responded.

"What is my purpose?" I asked. "Things have changed so much since we last spoke. I'm having trouble understanding anything that's happening."

Storm nodded in understanding.

"At first, everything seems unbelievable. Like an answer that is just beyond your mind's grasp," Storm said, confusing me even more.

"You've helped so much with our cause," Silver added.

"By showing Dane and Aneurin their real powers, we finally

have enough dragons to take on Freesia's Curse."

"So, that's it?" I said, dumbfounded. "I should just go back to my old life? What about the prophecy of me destroying it?"

Storm and Silver shared another look. In the space of their silence, I knew what they would tell me.

Zayda had surprised the holy hell out of me at the wedding. Her ability to sing Freesia's Song showed me that I wasn't alone in having extraordinary gifts.

"Your friend has great magic as well," Storm said. "Together, you were able to stop that small skirmish."

Skirmish?

I thought about all the people who were injured. No one had died, but we had been damn lucky. Some would be in the hospital for a long time recovering.

"If that's a skirmish, I would hate to see what the war's like," I said.

Storm and Silver both nodded.

"It is unclear how your powers fit into the future," Storm said. "But the emergence of your friend—the Blood Mage—has raised more questions than answers."

I wanted to press him for more information, but his attention was distracted.

Loch and Hael had ended their discussion and stood nearby. Dane and Aneurin were waiting as well.

"What is your answer?" Storm asked.

But did he really have to ask? Didn't he already know the future?

"Against our better judgment," Loch began, "we've agreed to join hordes. Only in the hope of ending this curse once and for all."

"Agreed," Aneurin said coldly.

"Very well," Storm responded. "Then it truly has begun."

CHAPTER 28: AN UNCERTAIN FUTURE

STORM

"Take the next few days to rest." My eyes looked at every face on the mountain, making sure that they were paying attention. "Prepare your bodies and your minds for a battle unlike any you've known before," I continued. "Xander and his army of dragon slayers have been waiting their entire lives for this moment."

"The fate of our species depends on it," added Silver.

The two hordes transformed back into their dragon forms. I felt a bubble of pride swell in my chest.

It had been stressful getting both sides to agree with this plan. In the end, they realized it was the only way for us to succeed.

Nothing guaranteed our victory for the future, but this was an excellent start.

Silver's fingers touched my shoulder, pulling me from my thoughts.

"I'm still worried," she admitted. "Are we certain this is the best plan of action?"

I dropped my head and met Silver's uncertain gaze. Even in times of indecision, she was as beautiful as ever.

"You know I can't decide the future," I said.

"This plan might fail. But there is only one way to find out."

The future was never guaranteed. Centuries in the Shadow Realm had proven as much.

Time and time again, we saw clouded visions. More than one promised an end to our suffering under the curse. Time and again, those visions were illusions; unfounded promises that led to false hope.

Rarely did I ever trust a vision completely. I could read the tea leaves better than anyone, but even I'd had my fair share of miscalculations.

In this instance...

The visions were actually coming true.

And I could only anticipate that the prophecy would become a reality.

The curse must be broken!

MADDIE

I might not be Freesia's second coming...

The thought was still hard to get over. For so long, Storm's words had led me to believe that I had the power to break the Curse.

Yes, he'd mentioned that I had a powerful friend. But I didn't really believe that her powers would be what ultimately ended the war.

Was I jealous?

It didn't really matter who ended the war, as long as Xander didn't win.

But I was a natural-born Dragon Slayer! It seemed like it was my destiny to destroy the curse.

Did Zayda already know?

She'd definitely had visions of Freesia's Song. It was possible that she'd already seen the future and knew how the curse would end.

Our relationship was already strained. Knowing that she had the power to end an entire war wouldn't help.

I thought back to the last civilized moments of the wedding. We'd almost fallen back into sync with one another.

Of course it would be our men's fault that our reunion was cut short.

Would we ever be able to recover even a spark of what we'd had before?

I was the one who had blasted the dragons out of the sky. But Storm seemed more interested in what Zayda had to offer.

When the time came, I would show everyone the power I possessed...

"It's time for your punishment, street rat," Loch drawled from somewhere behind me.

I had been staring out of the window of the penthouse, lost in all my troubles.

Little did I know, my biggest concern was in the same room.

Loch and Hael stood side-by-side, wearing nothing but their tight leather pants.

My eyes followed their giant statures, their bulging biceps and abs. Even when I knew the twins would punish me, I couldn't help but admire their godlike figures.

"And why the hell should I be punished?" I asked.

"You took something precious from us." Hael narrowed his sexy eyes on me. "And then you gave it to our sworn enemy."

Oh, yeah...

Everything moved at such a breakneck pace that I'd nearly forgotten about the Dragonstone.

I stood up from the couch and tried my best to muster the courage.

"That was for a very good reason," I retorted.

"And what reason was that?" Loch asked.

Would they believe that I did it to learn about my family?

I couldn't imagine that they even cared about family.

They'd lived on their own for so long.

"Personal reasons," I murmured.

"Isn't that wonderful," Hael replied, rolling his eyes. "Then we'll punish you for personal reasons as well."

They cornered me in the living room, blocking every path I had to escape. My actions had caught up with me. Shit, they were catching me acting all guilty.

I saw Loch brandish an odd-looking necklace with a bright red ball—and realized it was a gag...

I couldn't deny it was true to form, but they definitely didn't want me singing any songs that might knock them out.

The brothers weren't taking any risks.

They pounced on me like two jungle cats toying with their prey. I sidestepped Loch's groping hands and jumped over the couch, laughing.

Hael was ready and waiting, but I spun out of his path and headed down the hall.

The Dobrzyckas were fast, but they always underestimated me.

I sped down the hallway but quickly realized it would only lead to a dead end.

Damn it.

I was playing right into their hands.

They were allowing me to escape; pushing me exactly where they wanted.

I launched up the stairs to the second floor and sidestepped into their bedroom. I slammed the door and locked it behind me.

A lot of good that did...

Two puffs of smoke appeared behind me. Loch and Hael had me trapped.

There was one thing left to do.

I began to hum.

Loch lurched forward, trying to force the gag toward my mouth but it was already too late.

His legs weakened, and he stumbled to his knees.

Hael's eyes widened as he realized there was nothing he could do. I watched as he fell back onto the bed, giving in to the inevitable.

I continued to hum the melody as I pulled Loch to his feet. With careful steps, I moved him toward the bed and laid him on his back next to Hael.

I knew that Freesia's Song would knock them completely out...

That wasn't at all what I wanted.

"Are you two still able to put in some work?" I asked, feeling cheeky. "Or did my little song take all the fire out of you?"

In a matter of seconds, their leather pants dissipated into thin air. I bit my lip at the sight of their perfect physiques.

My hands ran down their abs, feeling every single lump of muscle. It was tempting to just jump on top and ride each of them until I blacked out from ecstasy.

But I wanted more than that.

I wanted control.

My hands grabbed each of their shafts and stroked them simultaneously.

"Don't tease us, little rat," Loch purred.

It was so *cute* hearing him object to something he had no control over.

"Be quiet," I smirked, kissing his legs. "It's time for me to have some fun."

I moved my attention to Hael and kissed the soft spot of his hips, causing him to flinch with pleasure.

My hands were sticky with their pre-cum, but I didn't want them to finish too soon.

I licked my tongue up the entire shaft of their cocks, taking joy as they each moaned.

I focused my mouth on Hael's cock while I positioned my hips over Loch's pulsing member. Deep moans escaped my lips as I slid Loch inside, feeling my pussy lips grip his shaft.

I gyrated my hips slowly while my tongue went wild on Hael's engorged tip.

His large hand grasped the back of my head and held it in place.

I gasped as the first waves of an orgasm overtook my body.

"Fuck me harder," Loch groaned.

Instead of bending to his will, I lifted my shaking legs off his dick and switched to Hael.

I fucked him harder, while I stared into Loch's lustful eyes.

"Did you want me to fuck you harder?" I teased. "But why would I? Hael's dick feels so much better."

I gripped Loch's shaft in my hand and leaned over, placing his entire sex in my mouth. I could taste my juices on his cock, and it made me go mad with desire.

My head moved up and down so quickly I couldn't imagine that Loch would last much longer.

Then, everything changed.

Loch pulled out of my mouth and was on his feet. A wicked smile spread across his face as I looked at him, confused.

"What the hell?" I asked.

I tried to climb off Hael, but his strong arms wrapped around me.

I couldn't move!

"You miscalculated the power of this song," Hael said.

"Now, we're in control," Loch chuckled deeply.

Still lying in bed, Hael thrust his hips up with a force I wasn't expecting. I couldn't do anything but rest my head on his chest as his massive dick fucked me senseless.

"I thought you wanted it harder," Hael said with a hiss.

I nodded my head, panting. I couldn't bring myself to speak.

Yes, fuck, yes. I want it so fucking hard.

"Don't forget about me," Loch whispered into my ear.

I felt his cock bounce playfully on my ass cheeks while I came over and over onto Hael's thrusting dick.

Without warning, Loch stuck his cock in my ass. A jolt of pain racked my body, and white spots danced across my vision.

But any discomfort I felt was immediately replaced with overwhelming euphoria.

I'd never felt pleasure like this in my entire life. The double penetration opened up a whole new world that I never knew existed.

From this position, Loch could hit my G-spot like it'd never been hit before.

Hael continued to hold me in place as Loch grabbed my hips. The brothers went to town on both of my holes as I ultimately submitted to their desires.

I had always imagined this and now it was finally happening.

I screamed from the mind-bending rapture.

"I'm...gonna...fucking...cum," I stammered.

Hael pulled me tighter to his body. Loch spanked my ass cheeks until I felt the burn.

Without realizing what I was doing, I placed a hand on my throbbing clit.

The combination of Loch hitting my G-spot through my ass, while Hael's rock-hard member fucked my pussy, sent me to orgasmic heaven. I was stretched to my limit.

When I added yet another dimension by rubbing my clit, my body went into full-blown convulsions.

I bucked like a wild horse as the brothers held on for dear life.

My eyes rolled back inside my head, and I lost all understanding of how the world worked.

All I knew was that I was cumming.

I couldn't stop.

I didn't want to stop.

I wanted to live in this feeling *forever*.

My pussy was enraptured in carnal bliss.

I felt my lips and ass clench tighter around their mountainous cocks while they both came inside me at the same time.

As each of them pulled free, convulsions trembled through my body.

Finished, I lay in between them in a total daze. Not long after, my eyes grew heavy, and I fell into a deep sleep. I had no words left.

I stood on the peak of the Dusk Mountains, staring into the sunless sky. It was the middle of the day, but the clouds were dark and ominous, blocking all light.

But as I continued looking at the sky, I realized there were no clouds at all.

The sun was being blotted by the giant bodies of dragons!

Thousands of them!

The sky ignited with a flash of light brighter than the sun. Dragonfire spread through the heavens, sending waves of heat washing over me.

Drops of rain suddenly dropped from the sky, breaking the unbearable heat.

I looked at my arms and nearly vomited from the sight.

It wasn't raining at all. It was BLOOD!

As the dragons flew closer, I opened my mouth to sing. It was all I could do. But my mouth was dry, and my voice was gone.

I couldn't even scream.

CHAPTER 29: BLOOD OF THE ROCK

SUMMER

The purple and orange of the setting sun made the sky look like a painting.

I'd chosen this section of the mountain as my own little haven.

Trees shielded it from the wind, while the cliffside offered a perfect view of the expanse of forest and hills.

It was ideal for thinking through problems or just getting some fresh air.

Dane and Aneurin had been cold and rigid since the meeting with Storm.

I knew that they had worries about joining with the Requiem horde.

I could understand why.

Maddie was always so sweet and thoughtful. When she visited the Dusk camp, it was like a breath of fresh air.

Her mates, on the other hand, both seemed like devils incarnate.

I heard someone approaching and felt a presence on either side of me.

"Hey, there, gorgeous," Dane said.

"We thought you might be here," Aneurin added.

I gave them each a kiss on the cheek as they sat down on the bench next to me.

"I was just trying to gather my thoughts," I admitted.

The brothers nodded without saying anything.

We turned our attention to the fiery orb of the sun as it continued its slow descent.

"I wish tomorrow would never come," Dane said.

"Same," Aneurin agreed.

This was the most they'd said since the meeting with Storm.

I wrapped an arm around each of their massive shoulders. It wasn't much help, but it was the least I could do.

They both leaned in closer, and I suddenly felt like some horny teenager at the movies, trying to hit on two dates at once.

But I didn't want them to leave. Their presence only made this fantastic moment more perfect.

"I'm terrified," I admitted. "Nothing about this feels right. We've only just met, and already our future together looks uncertain."

Dane's fingers gently touched my jaw and turned my head toward him. He kissed me on the lips, and I felt a million little sparks ignite throughout my body.

Aneurin kissed my neck, and I was overwhelmed with carnal passion.

I turned my attention to Aneurin and kissed him, allowing Dane to take his turn kissing my neck.

Summer: I don't want to lose either of you.

Dane: No matter what happens, we are yours.

Aneurin: Nothing can change that.

Summer: Promise me that everything will be okay.

Dane: I promise.

Aneurin: We'll never let anything hurt you.

I continued to kiss them as the last rays of the sun were extinguished below the horizon.

Their words gave me hope, but I knew it was only that—false expectations.

No matter how many promises they made, nothing was certain.

And I wasn't worried about anything happening to me. I'd lived my whole life being an abnormally healthy human being.

My extraordinary powers made more sense once I realized I could heal dragons...

But if tomorrow really was the beginning of an all-out war...I wasn't so sure my powers would be able to help...

XANDER

My footsteps echoed off the tile.

Scientists, doctors, and interns all nodded as I passed by.

All of my years of hard work were finally coming to a head. It had felt like ages ago that I had first set off on my journey as a dragon slayer.

Many young lives had been taken since the inception of Xander University. Many more would be lost in the coming days.

I entered a small room and smiled at the specimen sitting on the examining table, waiting for me.

"Xythor," I said. "It's so good to see you."

Xythor looked at me with amber eyes as warm as the sun. I

could understand why Zayda was so smitten with him—he was a beautiful being.

More so now that I'd given him an upgrade.

"It's good to see you too, master," he replied in a stoic tone.

During the processes of resurrection and reprogramming, I'd managed to add a few extra alterations.

Programming him to recognize me as his master was one of the best ones.

"I've heard all about your recent exploits," I said. "You really did a number on those Dobrzycka brothers."

I watched his eyes flash with rage upon hearing their names. Xythor had already held a particular disdain for Loch and Hael. All he needed was a few tweaks to make the thought of them nearly unbearable.

"My mission was to kill them, and I failed," he replied.

True, although it wasn't entirely his fault.

Up until the wedding, he had been programmed not to leave the university grounds. I'd set him free in hopes of learning how well he matched against real dragons.

In that regard, he did not disappoint.

If it weren't for Maddie and Zayda, he very well might have beaten them. While a living dragon grows tired over time, robot Xythor would not.

I moved to a nearby freezer and opened it up, releasing a puff of cold air. My eyes found the murky, red vial, and my fingers carefully removed it.

"Don't worry about failing," I said as I swirled the liquid in the tube. "There will be other chances to rip them apart. I have no doubt that you will complete your mission soon."

I moved to Xythor and gave him a sweet smile. Sure, I already had a son in Mason. But looking at him never gave me the same pleasure I had when I laid eyes on my greatest creation.

I touched Xythor's chiseled chest until I found the rigid outline of a door. I pressed a hidden button, and his chest opened up, revealing a compartment.

A golden glow emanated from inside. The small shard of Dragonstone was still in place and unharmed.

Next to it, however, was an empty vial.

I removed the empty glass and replaced it with the fresh, cold vial. The red liquid inside glowed ominously as the Dragonstone imbued it with golden light.

The Dragonstone alone was enough to give Xythor incredible strength and tenacity.

It was one of the main reasons we were able to bring him back to life.

When coupled with the Vitality Potion Zayda unwittingly helped me create from her blood, Xythor turned into a nearly impenetrable beast.

I closed the compartment and rubbed Xythor's cheek, feeling the warmth of his regenerated skin.

I couldn't quite place the feelings that welled up in my chest and stomach when I was around him.

Did I love this Frankenstein monster?

Did it matter? He was my creation and would do anything I told him to.

Unlike either of my actual children...

"They're coming for us," I said. "They think they can wipe us from this earth. But we will be more than ready."

Xander!

Xander!

I walked into the university's church and heard chants of my name echoing throughout the chapel.

The building was filled with students of Xander University. All of them had years of training as dragon slayers under their belts.

And all of them would follow their leader into battle.

I walked down the central aisle and watched as their faces beamed with utter jubilation.

On this campus, I was a god among mortals.

I made my way to the podium at the front and allowed them to bathe me with adulation and praise.

It never got too old hearing my name called out with joy over and over again.

In recent years, the chapel had become too small to hold the number of students that attended the services. Tonight, it was filled past capacity.

I looked around the stage and saw students sitting on the floor on either side of me.

Did they know how lucky they were?

Others would kill for a seat so close to their leader.

We'd placed safety mats on the floor so the students could safely listen to my speech without wading into the hot blood still dripping from Freesia's Rock. It wouldn't be good to have my potential soldiers injured from touching the toxic substance.

Over the past several days, the blood had spilled out onto more than half the campus, turning the pristine grounds into a sickening swamp. Although the students had grown worried that the entire university might be flooded, I couldn't be happier.

It was a beautiful sight that nearly brought me to tears.

Destiny was upon us.

I refocused my attention on the throng of students at the front of the chapel and raised my hands.

Their chants died down, replaced by absolute silence.

"It is a pleasure being here with you on this fateful night," I said.

Despite the mass of students, I could still hear my voice echoing off of the wooden rafters and walls.

"We are standing on the precipice of greatness," I continued. "The dragon hordes have no doubt banded together in hopes of overtaking us."

Boos began to rise from the students. I quickly held up my hands to quell the disturbance.

"You should be overjoyed," I said. "The prophecy is coming true. Soon...very soon...the dragons will descend upon the city."

I heard a few gasps, and they spurred me onward.

"Dragons will land on the outskirts of this campus and try to destroy us, one by one," I shouted. "But we will be prepared! We will fight until the very last dragon lays slaughtered in a pool of its own blood!"

The students erupted into cheers. Their exuberance was so loud that it caused the entire building to shake.

I heard a commotion behind me. It seemed like the students sitting on the stage were even more overwhelmed than the others.

I turned around to meet their smiles but was shocked by what I saw.

Freesia's Rock was no longer gushing blood. It was erupting like a volcano.

A few unlucky students were sitting too close and had been touched by the blood.

The cursed blood burned through their clothes and melted their skin. One poor boy's face was smoking from the acidic liquid.

I would act as if this was all part of the prophecy. The rock must be trying to meet our jubilant cheers with an eruption of blood.

But in reality, I was chilled to the bone.

It meant the dragons were gathering.

CHAPTER 30: DAY OF RECKONING

STORM

The beginning of the end was upon us. Dragons flew through the sky, choking the brightness of the midday sun. I hoped they would choose to rest and recharge. Perhaps they could revel in a beautiful sunset or enjoy a bountiful feast.

Sadly, for some, it would be their last day to do such things.

I watched as the Twin Leading Breeds from each horde transformed into their human bodies.

The four twins approached me but kept distance between themselves.

"We're here," Loch growled. "Though I'm still not sure why in the hell we agreed to this in the first place."

I smiled at his fake aggression. He could puff his chest all he wanted, but he knew as well as I how important today would be.

"You're here because your life depends on it," Dane replied

Loch looked as if he was about to lunge at the other set of twins. Hael placed a firm hand on his brother and held him back.

"If we beat Xander, there will be plenty of time to show them who really runs Requiem City," Hael replied.

Sadly, he was probably correct. Their alliance could only last for so long. If Xander was defeated, an all-out fight for supremacy of this region would take place.

Though if the curse was broken, the dragons would no longer be bound to this territory. With Xander gone, they could stretch their wings and fly to the ends of the earth.

Nothing would hold them back!

"Are you sure that we're ready?" Aneurin asked.

"It feels like only yesterday you taught us how to become dragons," Dane added. "Tell us the truth. Can we take on Xander and his school of slayers?"

They wanted the truth. But all I could give them was hope. The visions only showed me that we could make it this far.

It was now up to us to decide our fate.

"There is no more time," Silver said. "Unfortunately, providence does not wait for us."

Maddie and Summer had been talking in the distance, allowing their mates time to discuss the details of the battle. They walked up together, and I joined in on the discourse.

"Don't tell me you're actually scared," Maddie said.

She was looking at Loch and Hael with a devilish smile. Maddie had a strong will of her own, but even as she joked, I sensed an uneasiness in her voice.

"Quiet, rat," Hael growled.

"Don't talk to her like that," Summer replied.

Dane and Aneurin waved Summer to their side and placed her between them.

"Let them say what they will," Dane said. "They aren't fond of people trying to talk sense to them."

"The only talking we'll do is on the battlefield," Loch snarled. "Sure, you can run your mouths. But can you fight?"

"You've seen more than once what we're capable of," Aneurin responded.

"*Children!*" Silver shouted.

The four twins looked at her with disdain.

"Save yourselves for the dragon slayers," I said.

I looked at the position of the sun. It was at its zenith in the sky. We would need to move soon

"Ready your hordes," I warned. "The time has come."

MADDIE

I was as scared as I'd ever been. Hiding my fear behind a mask of belligerent pride had always helped.

But today just wasn't the same. Nothing I said or did felt right. The words I spoke every time I opened my mouth felt small and petty.

Hael and Loch were silent as we made our way back toward the Requiem horde. Without a word to anyone, they transformed into their giant dragon forms.

Loch: Climb onto my back mouse.

Maddie: Thought I was nothing but a rat.

Hael: You are whatever we say.

Maddie: Guys, I'm worried about today.

Loch: There's nothing to fear. This is our fate.

Hael: Climb on and hold tight. We won't tell you again.

Great.

I hoped this wasn't the last conversation we'd have. They were strong dragons who could hold their own, but what I saw during the wedding played in my head over and over. They were not the only ones who could put up a fight.

Please, please, don't let them die.

I didn't know who or what I was praying to. I just hoped that whatever heard me would listen.

I climbed up Loch's black scales and held on tight.

Summer was already on the back of Aneurin's dragon. She gave me a wave, and I happily returned it.

I'd finally found another woman who understood what I was going through. But if today went Xander's way, I'd probably never see her again.

I'd do everything in my power to prevent that from happening.

ZAYDA

Xander University was conspicuously quiet on the eve of a battle. Xander had tried to keep today's events a secret, but it was impossible to hide.

He'd taken the only man I'd ever loved from me. His own hands destroyed the panacea I'd worked my ass off to make. He even kidnapped me to keep me on his side.

And I'd let him...

But I refused to let him take Xythor to battle without saying one more goodbye.

I walked across the campus, assuming that Xythor was still in the laboratory. No one forbade me from setting foot on university grounds, but I still didn't want to be seen by Xander or any of his minions.

A group of students gathered outside the chapel caused me to stop and watch. They looked to be sharpening various swords and trying on suits of armor.

The preparation for battle had already begun.

I hid behind a statue of a dragon slayer felled long ago. It was enough to give me some concealment as I watched the students.

Xander wasn't anywhere to be seen.

But there was someone else I recognized...

Xythor!

His godlike figure would be hard to miss among such slender students.

I continued to watch him, unsure if I should allow myself to be seen. That was when I saw them...more robots!

Except these ones weren't like Xythor; there was no human element to their figures at all.

These robots were pure metal and already transformed into their dragon-like forms.

The blueprints I'd found in Xander's laboratory had been brought to life...

And they were fucking huge! My thoughts quickly drifted to Maddie and her mates. I hated Loch and Hael with a passion, that was no secret.

Still, I couldn't help but worry about what would happen to my friend if they were killed in this battle.

Maybe it was for the best...if dragons were wiped from this earth, who would shed a tear? My old friend, no doubt...

But her tears would only be used to water the new world Xander would create in their absence.

LOCH

We flew through the sky as one massive entity. Hael and I had never dreamed of building a horde.

Now that we had one, it was hard to deny the breathtaking power we possessed.

Storm: We're nearing the university!

Loch: How will we be able to enter? It's impossible with the curse.

Hael: Do you feel it? Something's different.

Silver: Hael's right. I can no longer sense the force field that usually encircles the campus.

Storm: Xander and his dragon slayers are waiting. They're calling us in…

We followed Storm as he made his descent.

For the first time in ages, I could feel my stomach twist into knots. The battle was nearing...and I didn't know if I was ready.

Maddie gripped my scales tightly, holding on for dear life.

I just hoped that I'd be able to feel her touch again after whatever happened next.

MADDIE

Loch touched down just outside the campus, and I jumped off. I sprinted toward the university's stone walls, not wanting to be left out of the fight.

Sooner or later, they would need me; I just knew it.

Summer eventually caught up and ran alongside me.

"This is fucking crazy," she said.

"Welcome to my life," I replied.

We found an open gate under an archway and followed it inside.

Just as we were about to make our plan of attack, a horrible, metallic roar filled the air.

"Holy hell," Summer said. "Look at that!"

I followed Summer's finger as she pointed to the sky.

Hordes of dragons were taking flight—and they weren't part of our dragon alliance.

They were robots!

My jaw dropped in terrified awe.

Xander really had been waiting all along for the Requiem and Dusk hordes to arrive.

How did he have so many dragons?

I grew instantly sick at the realization of my own question.

The Dragonstone...

In my pursuit to learn more about my mother, I'd handed over the one thing that Xander needed to defeat the dragons.

And it was all because of me.

I looked around the campus, trying to find a better vantage point.

On the other side of campus was a young woman staring at the sky just like Summer and I.

It was Zayda...

And she was on Xander's side.

I returned my attention to the sky. The hot afternoon sun was eclipsed by the dozens of dragons taking flight.

A battle was about to begin.

We'd all chosen our sides.

Next would come the fire, the blood, and the death.

Only one question remained...who would emerge from the ashes?

THANK YOU

Thank you for reading the Requiem City series.
You can find all other books of the series and hundreds of other bestsellers on the Galatea app.

Scan this QR code to download Galatea and use the code REQUIEMCITY20 to receive a 20% discount on the subscription.

Made in United States
Troutdale, OR
06/05/2024